The Elijah Project

The Chamber of Lies

Other Bill Myers Books You Will Enjoy

The Elijah Project
On The Run
The Enemy Closes In
Trapped by Shadows
The Chamber of Lies

The Forbidden Doors Series
The Dark Power Collection
The Invisible Terror Collection
The Deadly Loyalty Collection
The Ancient Forces Collection

Teen Nonfiction
The Dark Side of the Supernatural

The Elijah Project

The Chamber of Lies

Bill Myers
bestselling author

ZONDERVAN.com/
AUTHORTRACKER
follow your favorite authors

For Doc Hensley:

A teacher committed to truth.

ZONDERKIDZ

Chamber of Lies
Copyright © 2009 by Bill Myers

Requests for information should be addressed to:
Zonderkidz, *Grand Rapids, Michigan* 49530

Library of Congress Cataloging-in-Publication Data

Myers, Bill, 1953-
    Chamber of lies / by Bill Myers.
        p. cm. — (Elijah project ; bk. 4)
        Summary: Still trying to save his younger brother Elijah from the powers of darkness,
Zach must debate his faith with an expert atheist, while Elijah undergoes his own tests in the
sinister Chamber, which tempts him to deny God and follow the evil Shadow Man.
      ISBN 978-0-310-71196-4 (softcover)
      [1. Christian life — Fiction. 2. Supernatural — Fiction. 3. Adventure and
adventurers — Fiction. 4. Brothers and sisters — Fiction.] I. Title.
PZ7.M98234Ch 2009
[Fic] — dc22

2009001811

Published in association with the literary agency of Alive Communications, Inc.,
7680 Goddard Street #200, Colorado Springs CO 80920, www.alivecommunications.com.

Zonderkidz is a trademark of Zondervan.

Editor: Kathleen Kerr
Art direction: Merit Alderink
Cover illustration: Cliff Neilsen
Interior design: Carlos Eluterio Estrada

Printed in the United States of America

09 10 11 12 13 14 15 /DCI/ 20 19 18 17 16 15 14 13 12 11 10 9 8 7 6 5 4 3 2

Table of Contents

Consider it pure joy, my brothers, whenever you face trials of many kinds, because you know that the testing of your faith develops perseverance. Perseverance must finish its work so that you may be mature and complete, not lacking anything.

James 1:2–4

Chapter One

To the Rescue

"That's impossible!"

Willard looked up from the computer in the back of the rattling RV. "What is?" he asked.

"How can Elijah send us a message?" Thirteen-year-old Piper blew the hair out of her eyes. "He doesn't even know how to turn on a computer." She scowled back at the message on the monitor.

Don't try to save me!

Shadow Man has weapons you don't understand.

Elijah

Willard, Piper's geeky inventor friend, shoved up his glasses with his chubby sausage-like fingers. (Willard liked to eat more than your typical guy — actually, more than your typical *two* guys). "Run it past me again. Who exactly is this Shadow guy?"

"WHO isn't the right word," Piper said.

"More like *WHAT*," Zach, her sixteen-year-old brother, exclaimed. "We heard him speak back at Ashley's."

"Heard?" Willard asked, shoving up his glasses again.

"It's a long story, but believe me, the dude is not something you want to mess with."

"Everything all right back there?" Dad called from the driver's seat of the RV.

He and Mom sat up front as they drove through the twisting mountain road. The past few days had been rough on them. First, they'd had to leave the kids behind while they acted as decoys for the bad guys. Then they'd been kidnapped. Then they'd lost little Elijah. Then they'd wandered deep into mysterious caves and a cavern filled with strange supernatural beings. Definitely not good times. In fact, on the fun scale of 1–10 they were somewhere below 0.

But at least they had Piper and Zach, and their two friends, Willard and Cody. Together, the four kids sat at the back table.

"Don't worry about us," Zach called up to his parents, "everything's cool." He shot a look to Piper, telling her to keep quiet about the message on the computer screen. She couldn't have agreed more. After all that Mom and Dad had been through, they didn't need to worry about strange new weapons.

Suddenly, Dad hit the brakes and everyone flew forward.

Piper screamed and nearly hit her head on a cupboard, but Cody reached out and caught her in his arms. As the RV shuddered to a stop, he looked down at her and asked, "Are you okay?" His eyes were worried.

Piper gazed into his incredible blue eyes and half-croaked, "Yeah." She always half-croaked when she looked into his eyes. But it wasn't just his eyes. Everything about him made her a little unsteady on her feet (and a little fluttery in her heart).

Zach called up to Dad. "What's going on?"

"Looks like a detour," Dad said.

A sheriff approached the side door of the RV. Zach rose and opened it for him.

The man stuck his head inside. "Afternoon, folks."

Piper caught her breath. He looked exactly like the homeless person who had helped them in the streets of L.A.... and the customer who had helped them in the mountain restaurant ... and the angel who had fought for them in the cavern.

Piper stole a look to Zach. The way his mouth hung open, she knew he'd noticed it too.

"Is there a problem, Officer?" Dad asked.

The man nodded. "Highway is out. You'll have to turn around."

"But—"

"There's a dirt road about a mile back. It'll take you to where you're going."

Mom frowned. "How do you know where we're—"

"And be careful," he interrupted. "You folks still have plenty of dangers ahead. But you'll be okay. You've got plenty of folks looking out for you."

It was Dad's turn to frown. "I don't understand. 'Plenty of folks?'"

"That's our job," the officer smiled. "To look after the good guys." With that, he stepped back outside ... but not before catching Piper's eye and giving her a quick wink.

Piper could only stare. Who was this man? She moved to the window for a better view. But by the time she arrived, he was gone.

●

"They are coming thisss way."

Monica Specter stared across the picnic table to Shadow Man. Looking at the massive bulk of darkness always gave her the creeps. Actually, looking at him didn't give her the creeps, not being able to see him did. Well, at least not *all* of him. There was something strange about the way the man always sucked up light—even in the brightest day.

"Want I should hurt them?" Bruno, her brainless assistant, asked. He sat on the bench beside her. To make his point, he reached into his coat for his gun. A thoughtful gesture, if it hadn't been for the soda can sitting on the table beside him.

The soda can that he knocked over with his elbow.

The soda can that dumped its fizzy contents all over Monica's lap.

She leapt to her feet, wiping the soda away. "You idiot!"

"I'm sorry," he said. For a moment he looked puzzled, wondering if he should help her or use his gun to shoot the offending can.

Shadow Man saved him the trouble. With a wave of his arm, he sent Bruno's gun flying out of his hand and into the side of Monica's parked van. It gave an ominous *THUD* then fell to the ground.

"Your weaponsss are of no ussse," he hissed. "Not in thisss battle."

Monica glanced nervously at her two assistants: Bruno, who was as big as he was stupid, and Silas, who was as skinny as, well, as Bruno was stupid. The three of them had spent many days tracking down Elijah. And now, with the help of Shadow Man, they had finally captured him.

But instead of looking scared, the six-year-old sat on a nearby rock, humming happily to himself. Talk about strange.

Stranger still, Monica had never heard Elijah speak. In fact, she was beginning to wonder if he even knew how.

A low rumble filled the air. A vehicle was coming up the dirt road that they'd parked alongside.

"Is that them?" Silas asked.

Shadow Man grinned. "Yesss. They've come for the boy."

"Shouldn't we do something?" Monica screeched. (She didn't mean to screech; it was just her normal voice). "At least get the brat out of sight."

Shadow Man turned to look at her. At least she thought he was looking at her. It was hard to tell with his eyes always in shadows.

"After the accccident, I ssshall take care of the child. You three will ssstay behind and sssearch for sssurvivorsss."

"Accident?" Bruno said. "I don't see no accident."

"You will." Shadow Man smiled and for the briefest moment Monica thought she saw teeth ... or was it fangs? "You will."

The rumbling grew louder.

Shadow Man turned to Elijah. "Boy. To the vehicle."

Monica watched as Elijah rose and turned toward Shadow Man's enormous Hummer. The child's legs began walking, but they seemed to move against his will. He tried to stop, but one stiff step followed another until he arrived at the truck.

The driver, a huge bald man who stood guard, opened the back door.

Monica cleared her throat nervously. "Shouldn't we hide too? We're right next to the road, so they're bound to see us."

"There isss no need. The crasssh ssshall prevent it."

"But I don't see no crash," Bruno insisted.

"Watch and be amazzzed ..."

Chapter Two

The Crash

"Dad," Zach called from the back of the RV. "If this is a detour, how come we don't see any other cars? Or detour signs?"

"He's right," Mom agreed. "I've got a weird feeling about this."

Willard motioned to the computer monitor. "Check it out."

Zach looked down and saw the letters to another message appearing on the screen:

Deer coming from right.

Tell Dad to look out his window!

"Dad," Zach called. "Look to your right."

"What?"

"To your right! Look to your right. Now!"

Dad turned just in time to see four deer appear at the side of the road and dart in front of the RV. He cranked the wheel hard, veering to the left, barely missing them but sending the RV into a squealing skid.

●

Shadow Man watched with displeasure as the RV slid across the road, just missing the deer.

He turned to the Hummer and shouted at Elijah, "And you think that will ssstop me?!"

He raised his arm toward the cliff looming to the right over the roadway. Several giant boulders came loose and began to fall, bouncing toward the RV.

●

Zach was too busy fighting to keep his balance in the swerving RV to notice another message forming on the computer screen:

Rocks! Look out!

The first boulder slammed into the vehicle's side. The force was so powerful that it ripped the steering wheel out of Dad's hands. He grabbed it and fought to regain control of the vehicle. For a moment it looked like he had it, but then the second boulder hit. And then the third. And the fourth. The RV was batted around like a ping-pong ball as rocks continued to hit it.

"Hang on!" Dad shouted.

Dishes fell from the cupboard, crashing to the floor.

Everyone was yelling. Zach stumbled, tried to catch himself, and was thrown down.

But only for a second.

Before he realized what was happening, he was thrown into the left wall of the RV—then the roof.

They were rolling!

Bodies flew past him, legs kicking, people screaming. Glass exploded around him. There was more yelling as he hit the opposite wall, then finally the floor again.

Well, not actually the floor. More like Willard.

"Oaff!"

Zach landed on top of him, grateful for all the junk food and extra doughnuts the chubby kid had eaten, cushioning his fall.

"Sorry, Willard."

"That's ... okay ..." the kid groaned.

Zach scrambled back to his feet. He looked around to see if anyone was hurt. And then he saw Dad slumped over the wheel, blood trickling down the back of his head.

That's when he panicked. "Dad!'"

●

Monica watched with amazement as the big RV finished rolling and landed back on its wheels, filling the air with dust and smoke.

"Well, don't jussst ssstand there," Shadow Man hissed.

She turned to see the massive bulk of a man stepping into his Hummer.

"Go! Take care of the othersss!"

Monica wasn't exactly sure what he meant by "take care of," but she could make a good guess. She motioned to Silas and Bruno to follow her toward the RV.

"Grab your gun!" She pointed to Bruno's weapon lying next to her van where Shadow Man had flung it. "Don't forget your gun!"

●

As Piper staggered to her feet, she could hear Zach coughing and shouting, "Dad, are you all right?!"

She called out to her mother. "Mom, you okay?"

"Yes. It's just my leg. It's pinned against the dash, but I'm all right. How's everybody back there?"

Zach was crawling toward the front as Piper glanced to Cody and Willard. They were also rising to their feet. Cody was wincing, holding his right arm, but everyone else seemed okay.

"We're fine!" Piper shouted back.

She glanced around the RV. The kids may have been fine, but the place was a mess — dishes thrown out of the cupboard, everything tossed around and dumped on the floor. It was as bad as Zach's room.

Well, not quite, but close enough.

"How's Dad?" she called?"

"He's unconscious!" Zach shouted.

Piper sucked in her breath.

"It's the TV," Mom cried. "It fell off the shelf and hit the back of his head! Mike? Michael?"

Zach was kneeling beside him. "Dad, can you hear me?"

Piper's heart pounded as she moved forward to join them.

"Dad?"

She heard a groan and saw him move his head.

"He's coming around," Mom said. "Mike, can you hear me? Michael can—"

She was interrupted by the voice of a woman approaching from outside. "Anybody alive in there?"

Piper frowned. She'd heard that voice somewhere. More than once. But where? A second voice joined it.

"Want me to blow off the door?"

"Not yet, you idiot!" the woman screeched. "Try opening it first!"

"Oh, yeah." The man gave a nervous laugh. "Why didn't I think of that?"

Piper had her answer. There was no mistaking the rudeness of the woman—or the lack of intelligence of her assistant. And because of their missing manners (and brain cells) these were not people Piper wanted to meet again.

Zach must have recognized the voices too. "Dad," he said, "Dad, can you turn on the engine? Dad, can you get us out of here?"

But of course Dad couldn't. He was too busy just trying to open his eyes.

"Anybody in there?!" The woman's voice was much closer. Any second she'd open the door.

"Here," Zach said to his father, "let me scoot you over."

"What are you doing?" Mom asked.

He shifted Dad far enough to ease behind the wheel. He turned on the ignition. The motor ground away, but nothing happened. He tried again.

"Zach . . ."

He tried a third time, and the engine finally turned over. It wasn't happy about it, but at least it was running. And just in time.

Suddenly, the side door was yanked open, revealing a woman with flaming red hair. Beside her stood the biggest of her assistants. But they only stood there a second before Zach dropped the RV into gear, punched the accelerator, and took off.

"ZACH!" everyone shouted.

Well, everyone but the red-haired woman and her goon. It's hard to shout when you're busy leaping out of an RV doorway so your head doesn't get ripped off.

●

Shadow Man stared out his Hummer's window watching Monica and her bungling assistant start chasing after the RV. Despite dozens of dents, scratches, and broken windows, it still ran. This surprised Shadow Man and for a moment he didn't understand how it was possible.

Unless...

He stole a look at Elijah, who was seated at the back. Was this more of the boy's trickery? He knew the child had powers, but this?

Shadow Man couldn't be sure. All he knew was that the little brat was humming again. He hated it when the boy did that. He could make him stop, of course. But then the child would simply find some other way of trusting and thanking—of praising—the Enemy.

The Enemy. That was the whole reason Shadow Man was in this mess in the first place. The Enemy had finally started his preparation to bring about the end of days. And for some unknown reason he had chosen little Elijah as one of his most important tools in bringing about that end.

Shadow Man's lips curled into a tiny smile. Well, let the Enemy choose whom he would. And let the boy hum away, because very soon the child would turn his back on the Enemy. Very soon Shadow Man would bring Elijah over to his side of the battle, to where the real power lay.

All it would take was a little time in The Chamber. A little time to show the child the wonders and glories that would be his if he would deny the Enemy and follow Shadow Man's master.

Chapter Three

Decoy

"Where are they?" Zach shouted over the sputtering RV. He checked the cracked side mirrors for any sign of Monica or her assistant. "I don't see them!"

Cody called from the back window. "They've turned around. They're running back to their van!"

"Zach, slow down!" Mom cried.

"I will in just a second."

"We'll never get away!" Piper shouted. "Not in this thing. What do we do?"

"Hang on, I've got a plan."

"That's what I'm afraid of," she groaned. Piper always groaned when her big brother had a plan. Mostly because it was impossible to forget some of his more famous plans...

Like his plan to become a billionaire by selling bottles of air. Not fancy stuff like hospital oxygen bottles or anything like that. Just plain ol' air. "They do it with water," he reasoned. "So why not do it with air?"

Then there was his weight loss plan that involved eating ground up toe nail clippings mixed with slug slime. Actually, the eating wasn't too bad, it was the throwing up that wasn't so popular. In fact, the only bottle he ever sold was to Piper (which was how she knew about the throwing up).

His latest plan involved building an indoor swimming pool by shoving a hose under her bedroom door, taping up all the cracks around it and turning on the water. (If she hadn't opened her window, she would have drowned.) Good ol' Zach.

Fortunately, this plan worked just a little better. Well, sort of . . .

They rounded the bend and Zach pulled over to the side of the road, bringing the RV to a shuddering stop.

"What . . ." Dad coughed, "what are you doing?" He was still pretty out of it, but at least he could talk.

"We're going to lure them away from you guys," Zach said. "Away from the RV."

"What?" Mom asked.

"That will give you time to call 911 and get an ambulance up here for you and Dad."

"I'll be okay," Dad said, doing his best to sound all right but failing miserably.

"Yeah, right," Zach answered. He motioned for Piper, Willard, and Cody to head out the side door. "That van will be here any second. Come on, let's go!"

Normally, Piper would have put up a fuss. It made no difference whether it was a good plan or a bad plan. As the younger sister, she had to complain; it was an unspoken law. But at the moment, causing a diversion actually seemed like a pretty good idea—even if it was Zach's.

She stepped outside through the door. Willard and Cody followed.

Zach stayed inside just a second longer to talk to his parents. "Both of you keep your heads down so they can't see you. I'll lock this thing up. Once we're safe, we'll circle back around to make sure you've been picked up."

"Don't worry about us," Mom said. "I'll phone 911 and we'll be okay. But you be careful."

"Right—"

"I'm serious, Zachary ... be careful."

"Got it. I love you, Mom."

"I love you, too."

With that, Zach stepped out of the RV and locked the door—just as Monica and her van squealed around the corner.

By now Piper was standing at the edge of the woods. "Let's go," she motioned to her brother. "Come on, come on!"

"Not yet." Instead of joining her, Zach actually took a step closer to the road.

"What are you doing?!" she cried.

The van lurched and skidded to a stop fifty feet away.

"Zach!"

"Not yet."

The doors flew open and the red-haired woman and her two assistants piled out, both pointing guns.

"Zach!" Piper hissed.

"I want to make sure they see us."

The biggest goon was the first to fire, hitting a tree ten feet above Piper's head.

"They see us!" she cried.

"Good point!" Zach turned and sprinted toward her.

The second goon fired. This shot came a lot closer.

"Yes, they definitely see us!"

Zach, Piper, Willard, and Cody raced into the woods and disappeared. With any luck, the bad guys would follow.

●

"In here!" Shadow Man ordered. "Bring the boy into my officcce, and put him into The Chamber."

The bodyguard brought Elijah into Shadow Man's dark, wood-paneled office. At its very center sat a glass-enclosed case. The case was shaped like the bud of a flower and was only large enough for one person to stand inside.

As soon as Elijah saw it, his eyes widened.

Shadow Man gave a slow smile. The child could not possibly know what awaited him, but he obviously sensed the danger.

"Hold him!" Shadow Man ordered. "Don't let him go!"

The bodyguard gripped Elijah's arms tighter as he stooped down and shoved the boy into The Chamber.

Shadow Man could have used his powers to force the child inside, but those powers had been draining ever since they'd been away from the Compound. That's why they'd doubled back to return to his base of operation. Shadow Man drew his energy from the Compound. Actually, it was the cavern underneath the Compound. The cavern where the Supreme Master dwelled.

"Now leave usss," Shadow Man ordered.

The bodyguard nodded and stepped past Shadow

Man, keeping his eyes on the ground since he was never allowed to look at him. As the servant exited into the hallway, Shadow Man gave one final command.

"Ssshut the door."

The guard obeyed, slamming the door with a foreboding ... *BOOM!*

For a long moment Shadow Man remained motionless, staring at the boy. Hard to believe such a simple child would one day—one day soon—cause so much trouble. Still, children grow up. And since the Enemy's prophecies always come true, there was much to fear from this one.

He knew Elijah could not be killed. The Enemy would forbid it. He could not even be hurt. That was another promise the Enemy made to those who served him.

But the boy could be turned.

Not by force; it would have to be the child's own decision. But if Shadow Man could persuade Elijah to change his allegiance ... well now, that was another story.

And that was what The Chamber was all about.

Shadow Man approached the wall of the glass pod.

The boy was watching his every move—but not in fear. And it was this lack of fear that outraged Shadow Man. The Enemy's servants always seemed to serve him with such joy, even love. Shadow Man always served *his* master with cold, gut-twisting fear.

"Ssso, tell me, Elijah," he hissed. "Thisss God you follow." He was careful never to speak the Enemy's name. Speaking his name brought unbearable pain and drained Shadow Man of his power. "Don't you find it odd that he promisssesss to protect and defend you, yet your family isss conssstantly under attack?"

Elijah just stared at him through the glass.

"Haven't you ever imagined what your life would be like if you didn't follow thisss ssso called God of love? Haven't you ever imagined how much more fun you would have living like othersss? Being your own bosss? Doing whatever you like, whenever you want? You could finally be free. *Really* free."

Elijah started to smile.

Shadow Man fought back his irritation. The brat wouldn't be smiling for long.

He moved to a nearby pedestal. On top of it rested a strange sort of keyboard. "Imagination isss a powerful thing, young Elijah." He reached for the keys. "Just imagine what life would be like without your God. Better yet, imagine what my Massster could provide you. Unlimited fame. Unlimited popularity. Imagine being loved and adored by all who sssee you. He can give that to you. That and ssso much more."

The boy simply blinked.

"Are we having a hard time imagining that?"

Again, there was no answer.

Shadow Man reached for the keyboard. "Allow me to assissst you." His fingers flew across the keyboard. As they did, The Chamber grew brighter and brighter. A circular tube at the top began to pulsate: orange, red, green . . . orange, red, green . . . orange, red, green. . .

A strange look came over the child's eyes. They no longer blinked; they no longer moved.

Instead, they glazed over as the boy began to see the glorious future that could someday be his . . .

●

Bruno had been the first to enter the woods, followed by Monica, and finally Silas, who brought up the rear. They'd been going in this order for several minutes, and it seemed a fine idea.

K-THWACK!

Well, except for the branches.

K-THWACK! K-THWACK!

The ones that Bruno kept letting fly back and hitting Monica's—

K-THWACK! K-THWACK! K-THWACK!

—face.

Unable to take any more, she finally shrieked, "Bruno!"

He came to a stop and turned. "Huh?"

Trembling with rage, she pointed to the thin red scratches covering her cheeks and forehead.

"What happened to your face, Monica?" he asked. "It's all red and puffy."

She clenched her jaw, ready to explode.

"Are you allergic to something?"

Knowing she was about to blow a vessel, Silas stepped in and explained. "Yes, Bruno, she is allergic to something."

"What's that?"

"You!"

Bruno frowned. His bottom lip trembled. Then, just as he was about to break into a good cry, Silas noticed something on the ground.

"Look." He pointed to the footprints in the mud they'd been tracking. "They've split up. One set goes to the left, the other to the right."

"Oh no, what do we do?" Bruno cried. "They've outsmarted us!"

"Bruno."

"They've outfoxed us!"

"Bruno!"

"They've out—"

"BRUNO!"

The big man stopped.

Silas threw a glance to Monica. She was still trembling. That blood vessel could go any second, so he again explained. "There's three of us, right?

"Right."

"So we'll split up."

"Split up?"

"That's right."

Bruno's face brightened. "Oh, you mean one and a half of us will take the left path and one and a half of us will take the right?"

Silas glanced at Monica again.

She was feeling no better.

"Yeah," he said. "Something like that. But I've got a better plan. Why don't you head down the path to the right, and Monica and me, we'll take this one to the left."

"So we don't got to cut one of us in half?"

"Yeah," Silas nodded. "So we don't got to cut one of us in half."

"Cool," Bruno nodded. "I like that way lots better."

●

Zach had been the one to think of splitting up. That way if one group got caught, the other could still get away to help Mom and Dad—and Elijah.

Of course, his little sister, Piper, did her usual fretting and worrying, but eventually she agreed to follow the path to the right with Cody, while Zach and Willard went to the left.

That had been forty-five minutes ago, plenty of time for the ambulance to arrive and take Mom and Dad to the hospital. So now, according to Zach's plan, both his group and Piper's were circling back to the RV.

Everything was going perfectly...

Except for the gun that was suddenly pointed in Zach's face.

"Hold it right there."

Zach froze. It's hard to keep walking with a gun shoved in your face.

He wasn't sure how, but the skinny guy and red-haired woman had traveled through the brush and cut them off here on the trail.

"Now," the skinny guy said, "turn around nice and slow."

Zach and Willard obeyed.

"Did you honestly think you'd get away?" the red-haired woman sneered.

"You only got half of us," Zach shot back. "The others did get away."

"I wouldn't be so sure of that," the skinny guy answered. "We have someone hot on their trail."

Zach looked past him to see a big man lumbering up the path toward them. "You mean him?" he asked.

The red-haired woman turned and screeched, "Bruno?!"

"Present," the big man panted as he approached.

"What are you doing here?!"

"I gotta question."

"A question?!"

"When Silas said to take the right path, did he mean my right or his right?"

"My right or his right?! *My right or his right?!*—"

Zach noticed the woman's face getting strangely red, the veins in her neck starting to bulge.

That's when the skinny guy took over. "Actually, they're the same."

Bruno shook his head. "Nope. Cause when you face

me, your right is your left." He frowned. "Or is it my left is your right. No wait, a minute, I had this figured out a second ago. Your right is my —"

"Uh, Bruno?"

The big fellow looked to him, hopefully. "Yeah, Silas?"

The skinny guy took the big fellow's arm and turned him so they faced the same direction. "This is the path, correct?"

"Correct."

"And when we face the same direction, my right is exactly the same as your right. You see?" He tapped his right arm. "My right." He tapped the big guy's arm. "Your right. Exactly the same."

Bruno's face lit up like a kid who finally understood complex fractions. "That's ... amazing."

"I thought you'd appreciate it."

"You are so smart sometimes."

"Yes, well," he came to a stop. "What do you mean, 'sometimes?'"

But Bruno wasn't listening. He was too busy studying his arms. "Wow! Do other people know about this?"

"Just a few, Bruno. Just a few."

Silas turned back to Zach and Willard and sighed heavily. "Well, at least we've got you two."

"You want I should go after the others?" Bruno asked. "They'll be on my left, right?" He stopped and frowned.

Silas covered his eyes and looked to the ground.

The big guy continued. "Unless I turn the other way. Then they'll be, don't tell me now, then they'll be on my ..." He scratched his chin trying to figure it out.

Zach glanced toward the red-haired woman, who had dropped her head into her hands, slowly shaking it.

Then, before she exploded or the big guy could share any more brain bruising insights, her cell phone rang.

She pulled it from her pocket and looked at the number.

"It's Shadow Man," she murmured nervously. Opening it, she answered in her most pleasant voice, which still sounded a lot like fingernails on a blackboard.

"Yes, sir?"

The voice on the other end was so loud she had to hold the phone away from her ear. "Did you find them?"

"Uh, well, that is ..."

"It isss a sssimple quessstion. Are they in your posssesssion?"

"Uh, we have the children. But the parents are—"

"The parentsss are on the way to the Johnsssonville Hosssspital."

"The hospital?"

"My workersss there will handle them. But regarding the children ... I have far greater plansss for them."

"The children?" Monica asked. "*BOTH* children?"

"Yesss. I want you to contact Reverend Festool. Bring him in for a little chat with them."

Monica swallowed. Everyone in the group swallowed.

"What about their friends?" she asked.

All eyes shot to Willard, who would also have swallowed if his mouth hadn't become as dry as the Sahara Desert.

"Leave them. They are of no ussse. I want only the brother and sssisssster."

"The brother *and* sister?" Monica repeated.

"Yesss. The others will be free to live their pitiful

exissstence as they pleassse. But not the brother and ss-sissster."

"Got it," Monica said. "We're heading back to the van . . . with the brother *and* sister."

"Excccellent."

She slowly closed the phone.

"What do we do?" Silas asked. "We've only got the brother."

Monica glanced about the woods then sighed heavily. "Well, one is better than none. We'll keep lying and say we got both."

Silas gave her a look. "You know what will happen when he finds out."

"We'll cross that bridge when we come to it. Let's go." She started forward, giving Zach a push.

Silas motioned toward Willard. "What about Pills-bury Doughboy here?"

"Leave him," Monica called over her shoulder.

"But . . ." Willard whined. "You just can't leave me. How am I going to find my way back? It's getting dark and cold. What if I catch the sniffles? You wouldn't want me to catch the—"

"Silence!" the woman shouted.

Willard grew quiet.

Then, turning on her most pleasant voice (more fin-gernails on the blackboard) she said, "I assure you, you will not have to worry about any of those matters."

"I won't?" Willard asked nervously.

"Certainly not. The wild bears in these woods will make certain you never have to worry about anything again."

Chapter Four
Temptation

"What do we have here?" the doctor asked.

"Car accident," the ambulance attendant said. "Up on Bern Road." He continued pushing Dad's gurney down the hospital hallway.

Dad tried to lean up on one elbow. "Really, guys, I'm okay. I just got a little bump on the back of the head."

"Right," the doctor nodded, "but those little bumps can be nasty." He turned to the attendant. "Get him into the ER."

"ER?" the attendant asked. "If he's just got a little—"

"Did you hear what I said?"

"Right, but—"

"What about his wife?" the doctor asked. "You radioed that his wife was also—"

"I'm just a little bruised," Mom called from where she stood in the doorway. "I got my leg caught under the dashboard, but I'm fine."

"What are you doing standing?" the doctor demanded. "Somebody get her a wheelchair!"

"I'm fine, really."

"I'll be the judge of that."

Mom protested, "No, really, I'm not—"

"Is everybody questioning my authority today?" the doctor demanded.

"I'm not questioning your—"

"Will somebody *please* get this woman a wheelchair?!"

A nurse appeared from one of the rooms and scurried down the hall. "Yes, Doctor, right away."

●

"Shh." Cody motioned for Piper to press against the RV.

The voices approached from the other side. There was no mistaking who they belonged to or who they were talking with . . .

"You'll like Reverend Festool," the redheaded woman was saying. "He used to be one of you."

"What's that supposed to mean?" Zach asked.

"It means he also worked for the wrong side . . . until Shadow Man turned him—just like he'll turn you."

"Ooo, you've got me quaking in my boots," Zach answered.

Piper had heard enough. She started around the RV to help her brother until Cody grabbed her arm.

"What are you doing?" he whispered.

"Zach needs our help."

"They've got guns, remember?"

Reluctantly, she stopped as the voices passed by the other side. They were so close she could actually hear them breathing as the gravel crunched under their feet. There was one other sound—the faint clang of metal, which she could barely hear.

"Remember the last time we got together?" Zach was saying. He sounded just as cocky and overconfident as always. At least that's how he was pretending to sound. "Seems that one didn't exactly turn out the way you guys wanted, did it?"

"This time things will be different," one of the men answered. "Now that we've taken care of that little brat brother of yours."

Piper caught her breath. They were talking about Elijah. But what did they mean, "*taken care of*"?

As the voices headed toward the woman's van and started to fade, Piper felt herself trembling. The thought of losing one brother was bad enough. But two? Her eyes began burning and she gave them a quick swipe. Cody must have seen it for suddenly he was wrapping a warm, comforting arm around her.

"It's okay," he whispered. "We'll get them."

She looked up at his face. She wanted to ask how, and when, but her throat was so thick with emotion that she couldn't speak.

●

Elijah wasn't sure how he wound up on the giant stage screaming into the microphone. To be honest, he hardly spoke to anyone. But now he was singing to them, to thousands of them.

And they were loving it.

As he looked into the blinding lights he saw them screaming, shouting, trying to reach up to the stage to touch him. *Him!* Little Elijah Dawkins. Elijah Dawkins the runt. Elijah Dawkins, the boy nobody paid attention to.

He looked over to see his lead guitarist leap into the air, sweat flying off his body, as he made his instrument scream like some tortured animal. Off to his left, a keyboard player's long wet hair whipped back and forth as his fingers raced across the keyboard. Behind him, the drummer pounded out an intoxicating rhythm that shook the entire auditorium.

Elijah leaned back into the microphone and shouted out the next lyrics.

Guys pounded their fists into the air to the rhythm of the beat.

Girls screamed, fainted, held out their hands to him.

They all sang the words along with him, idolizing him, wanting to be him.

It was heaven. Better than heaven. One hundred thousand fans adoring him.

Loving him.

He caught a glimpse of himself on the giant TV screen above the stage. No longer was he little Elijah trapped in his puny body. With his shirt off, he looked incredible. Sweat glistening off his chest and bulging biceps, streams running down the chiseled muscles of his stomach. No wonder they loved him.

He looked like a god.

He pulled his focus back to the fans who were reaching up to him, begging him for the slightest touch. How could he refuse such devotion? Without hesitation, he ran to the edge of the stage and leapt into the air.

They would catch him, he knew it. They would do anything for him.

He landed on a hundred eager, outstretched hands, all grateful for the contact, all grateful to pass his body across the crowd, skimming their surface, like a surfer on the water.

So much adoration. So much love. So much worship.

And it was *all* for him.

●

Willard sat on a fallen log having a good old-fashioned pity party. Actually, he wasn't having the party yet. He was still working on the guest list, wondering which wild animal would be the first to eat him. It wasn't that Willard didn't like the wilderness. He just wasn't exactly an animal lover.

Some say it was because of the cute little puppy his parents bought him when he was four years old. The cute little puppy that loved to chew and tear up all Willard's favorite shoes ... especially when Willard was wearing them.

Others say it was from the ant farm that he slept with because he loved it so much ... until he accidentally rolled over and broke it. Actually, it wasn't the "breaking" that was difficult. It was the little critters crawling all over him as he slept that caused the problem—if you call six years of nightmares about being attacked by giant ants and five years of therapy a problem.

Finally, there was the incident of the sea gull landing on the patio bug zapper, spilling all the dead insects into his cup of chocolate milk. Unfortunately, nobody knew what happened until Willard started wondering why the chocolate milk had suddenly turned so crunchy.

All that to say, Willard was not thrilled with any

type of wildlife, bug or animal, crawly or crunchy. This would explain why he practically leaped out of his skin when a voice called to him from behind:

"Hey there, young fella."

"AUGH!" He spun around to see an old hermit, complete with a scraggy beard, approaching.

"Sorry." The old man chuckled. "Didn't mean to frighten you."

"Who ... who are you?"

"Who I am ain't important. But my problem is."

Willard checked out the old guy—plaid shirt, torn jeans, suspenders. He was so skinny a strong gust of wind would blow him over. Definitely not the kidnapper type. And definitely not a threat (unless he collected ants or had a bug zapper). Still, Willard wasn't going to take any chances. "What ... what type of problem?" he asked.

The old man approached. "You know anything about computers?"

"Well, yeah, that's kinda like my specialty." Willard pushed up his glasses and gave an asthmatic cough as if proving his point.

The hermit nodded. "Thing is, I got all this newfangled computer equipment in my cabin over yonder and I don't know the first thing 'bout using it."

"You have computer equipment?" Willard asked. "Out here?"

The man nodded. "Figured it's about time I enter the twentieth century."

"Actually," Willard corrected, "we're in the twenty-first century now."

"The twenty-first century! When did that happen?"

"Awhile back."

"Shoot. See how fast time flies when you ain't payin' attention?"

Willard gave half a nod.

"So you think you can help me out?"

Willard didn't answer, but continued staring at him. Because, despite the man's age, his scraggly beard, and worn clothes, there was something strangely familiar about him.

"Come on, son, we ain't got all day. It's gonna get dark soon."

Willard frowned, still trying to decide. He knew what his folks said about hanging out with strangers. But this guy was so old and frail that he couldn't possibly be dangerous. And he was right, it was getting dark—and cold.

"How ... how far is your cabin?"

"Just over yonder a piece."

Willard continued to think.

The old man gave a sigh. "Well, listen, if you ever decide to make up your mind," he turned and started back up the path, "just let me know and I'll—"

"No, wait!" Willard interrupted.

The man turned back.

Willard tried to sound less panicky. "What I mean is, I think I can squeeze you into my schedule."

The old-timer broke into a grin that showed more gums than teeth. "Well, that would be real neighborly." He turned and limped back up the path. "We'd best get a move on."

Willard scrambled to catch up.

"With any luck maybe we'll get inside 'fore supper time."

"Supper time?" Willard asked. "I wasn't planning on eating dinner with you."

"Oh, not me, son," the old man chuckled. "The animals.

With any luck, we'll get inside before they decide to have us for supper."

Willard nodded and picked up his pace.

●

"What are you doing to my husband?" Mom leapt from her wheelchair and started across the ER toward Dad.

"Grab her!" the doctor ordered.

The ambulance attendant reached out and caught Mom's arm, pulling her back to the chair. "Ma'am, you'll have to—"

"Let go of her!" Dad tried to rise from the gurney to help.

"Somebody hold him down!" the doctor yelled.

A big hulk of an intern pressed Dad's shoulders back onto the gurney.

"Get off me! Get—"

"Give me his arm!" the doctor yelled. "Hold it steady!"

The intern gripped Dad's arm and held it as the doctor prepared the hypodermic needle.

"Let go of me!" Mom yelled at the ambulance attendant. Then at the doctor. "What are you doing to him?!"

Dad continued to fight, but he was no match for the giant intern.

"What are you doing?!" Mom cried. "He doesn't need anything! He's just—"

The doctor inserted the needle into Dad's arm and emptied the syringe.

Mom went wild, "Mike, Mike . . ."

It was all the attendant could do to hold her in the chair.

"Michael!" She watched in horror as Dad's eyelids began to droop.

"It's all right," he mumbled. His whole body began to relax. "Everything's all ..." He closed his eyes. "Every ..." His jaw went slack and his head rolled to the side.

"Michael ...!"

But he no longer answered.

"What did you do?!" Mom yelled. "He didn't need that! It was just a bump on the head! What did you give him?!"

"Just a little something to help him sleep." The doctor reached for another syringe from a steel tray and crossed to her. "You seem a little tense as well, my dear."

"Tense! You just gave my husband a shot of who knows what! You bet I'm tense! And I'm mad! I'm real—"

"Yes," the doctor said, raising the syringe to the light and tapping out the air bubbles. "You must be going into shock from the accident." He came closer.

Mom grew cold. "What ... what are you doing?"

"I think you need something to help you relax."

"Relax! I don't need anything to relax!"

"Of course, you do. Just listen to yourself—shouting, screaming, near hysteria." He glanced toward the ambulance attendant. "Hold her good and tight."

The attendant protested, "But Doctor—"

"Do as I say or get out."

"But—"

The doctor had enough. He motioned over to the big intern to come and help with Mom. The man understood and joined them. He grabbed her shoulders and pressed her firmly into the chair.

"Let go of me! LET GO!"

The doctor swabbed her left arm. "This won't hurt a bit. I give you my word."

"LET GO OF—"

The needle punctured her skin and Mom felt a slight burn. She watched in shock as the syringe emptied into her arm. Again she tried squirming, kicking. But her body began to feel strangely heavy.

"Let go of ..."

Like Dad, her lids began to droop.

"There we go," the doctor said as he removed the syringe.

She looked up to him, saw him smiling down at her, his face blurring.

"That's it, just relax. Close your eyes."

She tried to keep them open, but they were so heavy.

"It really does no good to resist. Just relax."

Maybe he was right. Maybe closing them for just a second would help. She did, then immediately forced them back open. Now, the entire room was a blur. To clear it, she closed her eyes again.

This time, however, she did not have enough strength to reopen them. Or to remember why she wanted to.

Chapter Five

Dark Times

"What's this?" Cody bent to the ground and picked up the RV keys with his uninjured hand.

"I thought I heard Zach drop something," Piper said. "You think he did it on purpose?"

Cody headed for the door. "Well, he's definitely given us a way to rescue him."

"Right," Piper agreed as Cody shoved the key into the lock and it clicked open. "Now all we need to do is find them."

Cody pushed open the door, and they stepped into the RV. "It was a smart call getting an ambulance to pick up your folks," he said. "So was the idea of us splitting up and circling back."

Piper nodded. "Must be some kind of record."

"Record?"

"For Zach to be right two times in the same day."

For a second, Cody broke into that heartbreaker smile of his. Even now, even in this awful situation, Piper felt her stomach do a little flip-flop.

"Hey, check it out." Cody had made his way back to the table and the computer Willard had been using. "Looks like we got another message."

Piper joined him and read the monitor:

Guys, they got Zach.

IM me when you get this!

Willard.

Cody frowned. "I thought Willard was with them."

Piper slid behind the computer. "All we did was hear voices. We never saw any faces."

She reached for the keyboard and began to type. At least she tried. But with Cody watching she felt self-conscious and made tons of mistakes. Why did he have to keep watching when she needed to concentrate?

Finally, she got it right:

This is Piper. Where are you?

A moment later the answer appeared:

In the woods with some old hermit guy

and lots of very cool computer stuff.

"He's still in the woods?" Cody asked.

Piper typed:

You're right—they got Zach. Took him in their van.

We don't know where.

Almost immediately the answer came back:

This guy's got major state of the art stuff.

I can patch into satellites and search

the roads. They can't be far. Stand by.

Piper stared at the screen, then looked up to the driver's seat. Finally, she turned to Cody. "You think you can drive this thing?"

He held up his bad arm, wincing at the movement. "Not with this."

She blew the hair out of her eyes. "So even if we know where he is, we can't get to him."

"Why don't you drive?"

"I've never even driven a bumper car," she admitted.

"Then it's about time to learn."

She hesitated.

"Really, I can't drive like this," Cody said. "You're going to have to."

Piper wanted to fire off a snappy comeback, but it was hard to be clever when the little flip-flops in her stomach were tying it into one giant knot of fear.

●

Elijah looked out into the glaring lights and the mass of people shouting and screaming for his attention. The longer he looked, the deeper he saw into their hearts. And the deeper he saw, the more he realized the truth.

They weren't shouting and screaming for him—at least not on the inside. Something much greater was happening. Beyond the music. Beyond the concert. Deep inside their souls, a different screaming was going on.

Not for him, but for something much more serious. They were searching to fill their emptiness. To fill that awful loneliness they felt when they were by themselves, when they were alone in the silence, when they wondered if anybody really cared.

That was what Elijah saw as he looked into their faces, as he saw deep into their souls.

And that was what broke his heart.

He looked around the stage. The guitarist was still strangling the guitar. The keyboard player was still ripping up the keys. And the drummer was still pounded his drums with a passion that worked the crowd into a frenzy.

But it no longer meant anything—at least to Elijah. Now he saw the people's real need. Their emptiness. He knew there was nothing wrong with entertaining them, but he had so much more to offer. Instead of an hour's noise to drown out their emptiness, he would someday offer the power to fill it.

Forever.

In just a few years, when he was grown, he would be telling them about someone who would fill their hearts to overflowing. Someone who loved and adored them. Someone who would completely satisfy their hunger.

Compared to that, all this strutting and screaming meant nothing.

Now, at last, he understood.

Shadow Man thought he was tempting Elijah with fame and glory, but the temptation was nothing compared to what Elijah knew he could be doing for people in the future if he stayed true to what God wanted. Compared to that, this concert was worthless. This fame and glory was empty. It was as if Shadow Man was trying to convince Elijah to eat rubbish instead of the incredible banquet that had been prepared for him.

As understanding flooded Elijah's mind, the concert began to dissolve before his eyes. The music faded. The faces disappeared.

After a moment, he opened his eyes and found himself back inside The Chamber, all alone, staring out at Shadow Man. A very, very angry Shadow Man.

"Ssso, you think your powersss are greater than my Chamber, do you?"

Elijah was silent. He knew the truth, and that was all that mattered.

Shadow Man's fingers blurred across the control's keyboard as he typed in another new and tempting reality. "We ssshall sssee about that, young Elijah. For thisss is what you can be if you will deny your God and follow my Massster. Behold, and be amazzzed!"

Once again Elijah felt himself leaving the room. Once again he felt himself falling deep into his imagination.

The imagination of The Chamber. . .

●

The dingy motel room smelled of old carpet and stale smoke. The only good thing about it was that Zach was bigger than the cockroaches . . . well, most of them.

Monica and Silas had stepped out for a bite to eat. Bruno, the big guy, lay on the bed snoring up a storm. Just a few feet away, Zach sat at a rickety table sharing a pizza with Reverend Festool. He seemed a nice enough guy. Young, in good shape, funny. And the pizza he ordered, double-cheese with everything on it, wasn't half bad either.

"Let me get this straight," Festool said while chewing. "You and your folks think this little brother of yours is actually mentioned in the Bible?"

"Yeah, from what we can tell." Zach took a giant gulp of Coke and tried not to belch.

Festool laughed and shook his head as he reached for another slice of pizza. "That's too bad."

"Why's that?"

"Well, the Bible. I mean, let's face it." He took another bite. "We're talking about a book of fables that's thousands of years old. Don't tell me someone as smart as yourself buys into that stuff."

Zach lowered his cup. He'd been made fun of before for believing the Bible ... but not by a minister. "Don't you?" he asked.

Festool continued chewing. "Don't get me wrong, it's a great book, lots of good teaching ... but you don't actually believe all that stuff about people walking on water or raising folks from the dead."

Zach shrugged. "Why not? I mean, some things you just gotta believe cause of faith, right?"

Festool looked up from his pizza, a smear of grease shining on his chin. "Just like you believed in the tooth fairy?"

"That's completely different."

"How?"

"The Bible, well, it's the inspired word of God."

"Says who?"

"The Bible."

Festool broke out laughing.

Zach didn't.

Seeing the look on his face, Festool apologized. "I'm sorry. It's just, well, you're telling me the Bible is true because the Bible says it's true." He gave Zach a look. "Doesn't that strike you as just a little ... convenient?"

Zach felt his face start to redden.

Festool continued, an almost pitying look on his face. "That's like me telling you I'm president of the United States. And when you ask me to prove it, I say the proof is because I just told you."

Zach fidgeted. He was liking this conversation less and less. Come to think of it, the pizza wasn't so hot either.

Festool leaned toward Zach. "Seriously, let me ask you: what proof do you have that the Bible is even vaguely accurate — other than the fact that it says so?"

Zach's mind raced, trying to come up with an answer. All his life he'd been taught to believe in the Bible. That was what his parents believed, what his Sunday School teachers taught, and what his youth pastor preached.

But where was their proof?

Did they just believe because they were taught to believe? And if that's all he had to go on, then maybe Festool was right. Maybe believing in the Bible was no different than believing in Santa Claus or the Easter Bunny ... or the tooth fairy.

Festool lowered his voice, sounding more gentle. "Don't feel bad, Zach. There's nothing wrong with believing in the Bible or Jesus or God. Lots of good, decent people believe — especially children."

He wiped his chin with his napkin and continued.

"But as an adult, well, maybe it's time for you to put away childish things and start thinking like a grown-up."

Zach opened his mouth to answer, but he had none to give.

The Reverend pushed back his chair and stood. "Listen, I have some matters to attend to in town. But

I'll be back in a little while and we can continue our little discussion, okay?"

Zach stared at the table, barely hearing.

"Okay?"

He looked up to see the Reverend smiling down upon him. It was a kind smile. Gentle and understanding.

Ever so slightly, Zach began to nod. "Yeah. Sure."

Chapter Six
Wild Ride

"Look out!" Cody yelled, his hands clutching the armrests. "You're going the wrong way!"

Piper muttered angrily to herself. It wasn't her fault that Cody made her so nervous she'd shifted the RV into reverse instead of forward. Or that she'd pushed the gas instead of the brake.

"Stop! Left! Turn left!"

Or that when driving backwards her left was her right and her right was her—

"Look out!"

KERRRASH!

The good news? The RV finally came to a stop. The bad news was some poor tree had to sacrifice its life to make that possible.

Then, of course, there was the RV's back end. It probably wouldn't show from the roll Dad had given the RV earlier, but as a neat freak, Piper wasn't crazy about the giant dent she'd just put in it.

"I'm sorry..." She dropped her head onto the steering wheel—

HOOOOONK!

—then bolted back up.

"No, no, that's okay," Cody said as he crawled off the floor and back to his feet. "You did just fine."

"You're just saying that," she sniffed, wiping a sleeve across her eyes.

"No, really," he said, testing his arm to see how many more places he'd broken it. "For your first time, I think you did great."

She turned to him. "Really?"

She knew he was lying came when he tried to smile but couldn't quite pull it off. His lips turned up at the corners, but his eyes darted back and forth like a caged turkey on Thanksgiving morning.

"I guess ..." she sniffed and reached for the gear shift. "I guess I'd better try again."

The second sign that he was lying came when his voice got higher and cracked like a thirteen-year-old boy going through puberty.

"Wait just a second!" he croaked. Forcing himself to calm down, he continued. "You know, until we catch our breath."

Piper gave him a look.

He gave her a weak smile.

●

Zach sat at the table staring at the unfinished pizza. The words the Reverend had spoken earlier still haunted him and he didn't feel much like eating ... which was a first as far as he could remember.

There was a knock at the door, and a voice called out, "Housekeeping."

Bruno got up from watching a rerun of *The Brady Bunch* and opened the door. An aging, disheveled man stood in the hall beside a rollaway bed, "You order an extra cot?" he asked.

Bruno looked over to Silas who was now asleep on the sofa, then to Monica who was sprawled out on the bed. "Uh, I don't think so."

"How many you got in here?" the man asked.

Bruno scratched his head. "Just the three of us. Oh, and the boy at the table that we ain't supposed to tell nobody about."

The janitor nodded. "Ah, then it must be for him." He entered the room and rolled the bed toward the table.

Zach looked up numbly and watched. There was something strangely familiar about the man, but he couldn't place it. Bruno hobbled back to the TV to continue watching *The Brady Bunch* marathon as the janitor opened the cot for Zach.

There, lying in its center, was a cell phone.

"What's that?" Zack asked.

The janitor picked it up and frowned. "Must be left over from the last guest." He tossed it to Zach.

"Don't you want it?" Zach asked, "In case they come back to claim it?"

The janitor shook his head. "Nobody will come back for that."

"How do you know?"

"I know." He held Zach's eyes a moment, and suddenly Zach remembered. The man's eyes were the same as the sheriff's who had sent them on the detour.

The janitor glanced over to Monica, Silas, and Bruno, then back to Zach. He lowered his voice. "You won't be able to make any calls, but you may receive some interesting e-mails."

Zach's mouth dropped open. He had a thousand things to ask. Unfortunately, all that came out was "But ..."

The old man headed for the door.

"But ... but ..."

He turned the knob and opened it.

"But ... but ... but ... "

He looked back and interrupted Zach's motorboat imitation. "Everything will be okay, Son. You just keep trusting God, and everything will be all right." He gave a wink, stepped outside and gently closed the door.

●

The computer equipment was incredible. Everything was top of the line. There were even a few extras that Willard hadn't known existed. He had no trouble tracking Monica and her thugs to a Motel 3 (they were too cheap for a Motel 6). Once he found the address he sent it to Piper and Cody.

Apparently, the two had been having a little trouble driving the RV (Piper refused to give details), but it sounded like everything was going better now.

Willard hoped so. He knew Piper could be the shy type and not talk a lot. He also knew she was crazy over his friend, Cody. Nothing obvious. Just little things like forgetting what she was saying when she looked at him.

Becoming super clumsy. And always pushing her hair behind her ears or blowing it out of her eyes.

Of course, Cody never noticed any of that. There he was, the best looking guy in the school. All the girls flirted with him to his face and sighed longingly behind his back—and yet he was totally clueless. Maybe that was one of the things they liked about him. He had no idea how cool he was.

But Willard didn't have that trouble. He knew exactly how UNcool he was. No girl ever flirted with him to his face (unless you call making up excuses for running away "flirting,") and they *definitely* never sighed behind his back (unless it came with all their giggling and eye-rolling).

Why someone like Cody would ever hang out with someone like him was beyond reason. But they'd been friends ever since they were little kids. And that was another cool thing about Cody. He never forgot his friends.

Back at the cabin, Willard had barely finished sending out the information over the computer before the hermit opened the door and stepped inside.

"Where have you been?" Willard asked.

"Had a couple of loose ends to tie up. How's it goin' with you?"

"I just sent the address to Piper and Cody. They should—"

One of the computer screens flickered, and Willard turned to look at it. "What's going on?"

The old man hobbled to his side. "What?"

Willard stared at the screen. It was filled with all sorts of writing. It seemed to be mostly historical and archaeological stuff. "How'd that get on there?" he asked.

The hermit leaned toward the screen. "Hmm ...
What's that say at the bottom?"

Willard read the final sentence:

"Please send by pressing *enter*."

The old man reached past Willard and hit the key.

"What are you doing?" Willard asked.

The old guy shrugged. "It said to press *enter*, so I
figured we should press *enter*."

"But you don't even know who it's from—or where
it's going."

Again the hermit shrugged. "If there's one thing
I learned about these newfangled computers, it's that
when they want somethin', it's usually best not to argue
with 'em."

Willard looked at the screen then let out a weary sigh.
The old timer obviously didn't know what he was doing.
Then again, most of the time, neither did Willard.

●

It was getting late. Maybe the Reverend wouldn't be
coming back after all. At least that's what Zach hoped.
Their last discussion really got him to thinking. And to
doubting. Maybe the guy was right. Maybe you really
couldn't trust the Bible was accurate. Just because he
learned it in Sunday school didn't necessarily make it
true. Or did it?

A few moments later he felt the cell phone vibrate
in his pocket. He reached for it, glancing around the
motel room to make sure everyone was watching *The
Brady Brides Reunion* (Bruno sure liked his *Brady Bunch*).

When he was sure the coast was clear, he pulled out the phone and read the subject on the screen:

"Some Arguments Proving the Accuracy of the Bible"

He scrolled down and read:

FACT

Jesus Christ believed the Scriptures and often quoted from them.

FACT

Archaeologists have used the Bible to discover over 200 ancient locations. Every few years another discovery is made that proves the absolute historical accuracy of Scripture.

Zach caught his breath. It was like the screen was answering the very questions Reverend Festool had raised. He scrolled down to read more:

FACT

Other historians who lived around the time of Christ also wrote about Jesus, supporting what was recorded in the Bible. In fact, there are so many historical writings about Christ outside of the Bible that it is possible to construct His entire life without ever going to the Bible.

Zach's heart pounded. There was more:

FACT

Here is an example from the famous Jewish historian

named Josephus who lived back in the First Century. None of his writings are in the Bible.

"Now there was about this time Jesus, a wise man, if it be lawful to call him a man, for he was a doer of wonderful works, a teacher of such men as receive the truth with pleasure. He drew over to himself both many of the Jews and many of the Gentiles. He was the Christ and when Pilate, at the suggestion of the principal men among us, had condemned him to the cross, those that loved him at the first did not forsake him; for he appeared to them alive again on the third day; as the divine prophets had foretold these and ten thousand other wonderful things concerning him. And the tribe of Christians so named from him are not extinct at this day."

Zach couldn't believe his eyes. He especially liked the part about being called a *"tribe of Christians."* But he had no sooner finished reading before there was a knock on the door.

Monica rose from the sofa, crossed to the door and gave her usual screeching, "Who is it?"

"Reverend Festool," came the reply.

She unlocked the door and opened it. Then, in her ever-pleasant manner, she turned without a word and headed back to watch TV.

The Reverend entered and nodded to Zach. "So, have you given any more thought to what we were discussing earlier?"

"Yeah," Zach coughed slightly as he slipped the cell phone into his pocket. "I sure have."

"Good," the Reverend pulled up a chair. "So tell me, as a bright and intelligent young man, what conclusions have you come to?" He gave his usual smile.

Zach pulled up his own chair. He took a deep breath and began, somehow figuring Reverend Festool wouldn't be smiling quite as big when he heard the information.

Chapter Seven

To the Rescue Again—Sorta

Elijah felt the football snap into his little hands. Only they weren't so little anymore. Now they were a man's hands. A BIG man's hands.

He dropped back from the line of players, his muscular legs powerful and poised for action.

He was no longer wimpy little Elijah, the pip-squeak that everybody made fun of. Thanks to The Chamber he now towered six feet five inches high and had the body of a superstar athlete.

He glanced to the turf below and saw the Superbowl logo. He was the star quarterback playing the Superbowl!

The stadium was packed with cheering fans. But it

wasn't the fans that thrilled him. He'd overcome wanting to be loved by the masses back at the concert. Instead, it was the power of his new, magnificent body.

He looked downfield and saw his receivers trying to break free from the defense, trying to open themselves up for a pass.

He glanced to the scoreboard: 14 to 14 with eight seconds left in the game.

This was the final play. It all depended on him.

Two giant linemen, 300 pounds each, broke through the line and charged toward him.

He looked back downfield. His teammates still weren't open.

There was only one choice.

Tucking the ball under his massive arm, the mighty Elijah pivoted to the right and broke toward the left, heading for the only opening he saw.

But that opening was immediately filled by another giant opponent who charged toward him. Still, he was no match for Elijah's speed and agility. Elijah faked to the right and continued to the left. The giant lunged and grabbed his jersey, but Elijah spun free and raced through the hole.

More arms reached for him, a pair grabbed at his legs, but he leaped away and continued running.

A tunnel formed ahead of him. His blockers were finally clearing a path.

His legs pumped as he sprinted forward. He would have to push his body to the very edge, but that was what it was for.

Another player came at him from the left. Elijah turned on the afterburners and jetted away like a rocket. Nothing could stop him!

The goalposts shimmered 60 yards ahead!

The tunnel narrowed. He picked up speed. There was no end to his power.

50 yards.

The crowd was on their feet roaring.

40 yards.

Adrenaline pumped; his heart pounded.

30 yards.

The roar was deafening.

He could go on like this forever. What a fantastic body, what awesome power! He had never imagined this strength and power—and now it was all his!

●

The good news was that Piper had finally managed to shift the RV into forward. The bad news was, well, that Piper had finally shifted the RV into forward.

Minutes later, thanks to Willard's directions, they were heading down the mountain road to Motel 3 to rescue Zach. She wasn't exactly sure what they'd do once they found him. Or how to find Elijah. Or how to find her parents.

But, at the moment, none of that mattered, because right now she had other things on her mind like...

"LOOK OUT! TURN RIGHT!"

... staying alive.

She yanked the wheel to the right, pulling the RV back into her lane and out of the oncoming traffic with the approaching...

HONKKKK

... semi truck.

It was a good move.

What was *not* so good was when she turned too hard, which meant she not only swerved to her side of the road, but also beyond ... toward the 800-foot drop-off directly in front of them.

"LEFT!" Cody shouted, grabbing at the wheel with his good arm. "TURN LEFT!"

"Left! Right! Make up your mind!" Piper yelled as she cranked the wheel hard to the left and barely missed the drop-off.

Unfortunately, she cranked too hard, swerving back into the wrong lane, and right into the path of the school bus loaded with kids.

"AUGH!" Cody yelled.

"AUGH!" Piper replied.

"AUGHHHHHHHHHHHH!" the kids agreed.

Once again Piper yanked the wheel, and once again she barely missed death, though the side mirror on the school bus wasn't so—

CRUNCH!

—lucky.

"How many more miles?" Piper asked, a note of desperation in her voice.

Cody didn't answer.

"How many more—?" She turned to him and stopped. She figured it was rude to interrupt someone whose eyes were closed and who was praying for his life.

Not that she blamed him. In fact, it made so much sense that she turned back to the road and tried it too. Not that she closed her eyes (though at this rate she wasn't sure how much difference it would make).

But she did start to pray.

●

Reverend Festool was pretty steamed when Zach gave him the answers that offered proof of the Bible's accuracy. But it didn't stop him. Instead, he came at Zach with a whole new argument.

"What about Jesus?"

"What do you mean?" Zach asked.

"So what if the Bible accurately recorded what he said and did. What if he was lying? What if he was just out to fool people?"

Zach looked at the Reverend. It was another good point. Even if the Bible did quote Jesus correctly and even if it did report his miracles ... what if he was just a liar? What if all Jesus' miracles were nothing but a bunch of magic tricks to fool people?

Before Zach could answer, he felt the cell phone in his pants pocket start to vibrate.

"Uh, excuse me." He rose from the table. "I need to use the bathroom for a sec."

"Take your time," the Reverend said. "And think about what I've been saying." He gave Zach a smile. "After all, these are very important questions."

●

The roar of the crowd filled Elijah's ears. Just a few more yards and he would cross the goal line and win the Superbowl!

He didn't know how much of his magnificent body was his imagination or how much of it had become real. But, even as he ran toward the end zone, he began to wonder how long it would last. How long would he be in such fabulous shape? Ten years? Twenty? Sure, that was a long time, but it wasn't forever.

Because everybody gets old. And everybody dies.

The goal line lay 20 yards ahead.

He remembered his grandfather, another great athlete, strong as an ox. He also remembered him dying last year as a shriveled old man. Then there was Elijah's father. Even he was starting to get old. It happened to everybody. As great as Elijah's body was, it wouldn't last forever. Nothing lasted forever.

15 yards to go.

But that wasn't true. There *was* something that lasted forever. If he obeyed God, there were the people he would touch. The people he would lead to God. The people whose lives would be changed—forever.

10 yards.

Sure, he could have the fantastic body now and get all the trophies and awards. But in a few years, who would remember? Or care? And after that? After he was dead? It's not like he could pack his fancy body and trophies into a coffin and take them to heaven.

5 yards.

But changed lives—those he *could* take to heaven. And if he obeyed, if he did what God wanted him to, there would be thousands of those lives.

Suddenly, the choice appeared very easy. A moment of greatness now, or an eternity of greatness later?

Elijah made up his mind. As he did, the roar of the crowd started to fade. He dug his cleats into the turf and veered to the right. Instead of crossing the goal line, he headed off the field. Only it was no longer a field. Now it was turning into a smooth floor.

The floor of The Chamber.

His powerful legs continued to drive his body toward the stadium's exit. Only it was no longer a stadium. Now it was becoming the glass case.

But he did not stop. He lowered his shoulder and slammed into the glass. It shattered and fell all around him.

"Look what you've done!" Shadow Man shouted. "Look what you've done!"

Elijah knew his body had never changed, that it was all in his imagination, in his mind . . . but his body didn't know it, not yet. Still, thinking he was strong, he leapt from The Chamber and raced past Shadow Man toward the door. But before he even arrived, the big bodyguard appeared blocking his exit.

Or at least he tried.

Remembering his moves on the field, Elijah faked to the right, and the big man lunged for him. Then Elijah pivoted to the left and slipped past the man and sprinted down the hallway.

"Ssstop him!" Shadow Man screamed. "Don't let him get away!"

Elijah began wheezing, trying to catch his breath. Making fancy moves was one thing. But he was not the mighty man who could run forever. He was just the wimpy boy. Still, he would not stop. At the end of the hall, he saw a door and, beyond that, freedom.

"SSSSTOP HIM!"

Elijah's lungs were on fire. His legs felt like rubber. The edges around his vision started to turn white. He was going to pass out.

Still he ran.

He stumbled into the door and opened it. Fresh night air struck his face. An alarm began to sound. Guard dogs barked.

Where should he run? What direction?

He paused, waiting for an impression, waiting to hear that still small voice that so often directed him.

Into the woods.

He turned and staggered toward the forest.

●

"He gave us the wrong directions!" Piper shouted. "There's no way this road leads to any motel!"

Cody nodded and quickly typed into the computer:

Willard where are we? You told us the wrong way!

For the most part, Piper's driving had improved. Even in the early evening with her headlights on, she managed to stay on her side of the road. Most of the time. More importantly, she hadn't killed anyone—yet. If anybody needed proof that prayer really did work, she had it.

Now they were driving through the forest on a dirt road. There were more than enough dips—

SLAM

"AUGH!"

—and pot holes.

"YIKES!"

But somehow the broken-down RV just kept going. The fact that Piper was able to avoid hitting any more trees also came in handy. The fact that a squirrel darted out in front of her, was not.

"HANG ON!" she shouted.

She yanked the wheel hard to the right and the RV did the usual skidding and sliding out of control while the kids inside did their usual screaming and shouting for their lives.

"AUUUUGH!"

But somehow Piper straightened them out and they kept going.

She looked to the rearview mirror and called back to Cody. "Any news from Willard?"

"Something's coming in!" He shouted up to her.

"What's he say?"

"Hang on!"

"Tell him it looks like he's got us heading back to Shadow Man's headquarters!"

"Oh, brother!"

Piper looked back into the mirror. "What?"

"We've lost the connection."

"Not now!"

Cody shook his head. "There's no signal."

Piper sighed and whispered under her breath. "God, what are you doing? Why aren't you helping us?"

"To the right!" Cody shouted. He pointed out the window into the darkness. "What's that in the field to our right?"

Piper glanced from the road to an approaching field. A person was running, stumbling in the moonlight. A little person.

"Elijah!" Cody shouted. "It's Elijah!"

Piper's heart skipped a beat.

Cody pressed his face against the cold glass. "Oh no!" he shouted.

"What?"

"There's a bunch of guys after him."

"Guys?" Piper asked.

"Yeah. And dogs!"

Without word, Piper cranked the wheel hard to the right. They bounced off the road and into the open field. Now they were heading straight for Elijah.

Chapter Eight
Pick up and Delivery

People never look their best when they're angry. Reverend Festool proved this with his red face and bulging eyeballs. "I have studied all of my life," he sputtered. "I have a Ph.D. in theology. How do you, a mere child, know these things?"

Zach shrugged. "Guess I just did my homework. Oh, and did you also know that Jesus fulfilled over 300 prophecies about himself in the Bible? Some of them were written hundreds, even thousands, of years before he was even born."

The Reverend's face grew redder.

Earlier, when Zach was in the bathroom, he'd memorized the information that came in over his cell phone. Now he was reciting it as quickly as he could, before he forgot.

"Those prophecies included everything from his birth in Bethlehem, to going to Egypt, to his healing people, to his death on the cross between two thieves, to his resurrection, and on and on."

"He could have manipulated those things," Festool said, "to fulfill those prophecies!"

Zach smiled. "Maybe. But the chances of one person fulfilling only the top eight prophecies about Jesus in the Bible are something like one in one hundred quadrillion."

"You're . . . you're making that up."

"Nope. Those are the same odds you'd get if you covered the whole state of Texas with silver dollars two feet deep, painted one red, tossed it in the center, stirred up the pile, and gave a blind man one chance to pick out the red one."

"That's impossible!" Festool shouted. He was so worked up that he even managed to draw Monica and her thugs away from *The Brady Grandchildren Revisited*.

"You're right," Zach agreed. "That is impossible. Unless, of course, he really was who he said he was. Unless, he really was God."

"No," Festool was on his feet. "He was a good teacher, I'll give you that, but he certainly wasn't God!"

"Wrong again. Jesus claimed to be God over and over. A good teacher wouldn't claim that. Maybe a con artist. Maybe a nut case. But no way would a good teacher claim to be God—unless, of course, he really was."

"This is ridiculous!" Festool sputtered. "I don't have to stand for this."

He turned and started toward the door.

"Where do you think you're going?" Monica shouted.

"I'll not be instructed by a mere boy." He opened the door.

Monica headed toward him. "Shadow Man gave you direct orders."

Festool came to a stop.

"You would dare defy him?"

"Well, no. I ... I ..."

"You have a job to do; I suggest you finish it."

"But—"

"Shadow Man is turning his brat of a brother at the Compound. Your orders are to turn this one. If you don't, there will be serious consequences."

Festool hesitated.

"And I think you know what I mean by *serious.*"

The Reverend wilted. He turned and shuffled slowly back to the table. Fortunately, he was so distraught that he forgot to close the door, leaving it wide open. That was his big mistake.

And Zach's big break.

Zach leapt up and raced for the doorway. Monica lunged for him but grabbed only air as he ran outside into the night.

"After him!" Monica screeched.

Zach darted through the parking lot, looking for some way out. Unfortunately, the only way came in the form of a burly, tattooed biker standing a few yards from his monster bike, trying to impress a burly, tattooed woman.

Zach raced to the bike and hopped on.

"HEY!" Burly Guy shouted. "What are you doing with my bike!"

"Sorry!" Zach yelled as he hit start and the engine kicked over. "I'll bring it back, I promise!"

The good news was the biker was so heavy, it took him 7 ½ seconds to lumber over to the bike.

The better news was Zach had the bike off its stand and the engine revved in 5 ¼ seconds.

The bad news was the bike was a lot more powerful than Zach's motor scooter at home.

So powerful, and with such awesome acceleration, that Zach could barely control his wheelie and, of course, his hysterical screaming.

•

"Closer!" Cody shouted to Piper from the RV's open door. "I can't reach him! Closer!"

Piper kept a careful eye on the side mirror as she brought the moving RV beside her running brother. If they'd had time, she would have stopped. But the guards were quickly closing in and the two German shepherds were already at Elijah's heels, snapping away.

The RV leaped and bucked as it hit ruts and holes. More than once, the wheel nearly jerked out of Piper's hands. But she held on tight. This was her little brother they were trying to save, and nothing would make her let go.

"Closer!" Cody yelled.

The dogs were right there. She could hear their growls and snarls.

"Closer!"

Another series of bumps, but she held on.

"Closer ... closer ... GOT HIM!"

She glanced in the mirror and saw Cody pulling Elijah into the RV. She figured the weight was probably killing Cody's bad arm, but he didn't complain. She was surprised that she still heard snarling and growling until she saw that the dog had latched its jaws onto Elijah's pant leg and wouldn't let go, even if it meant being hauled on board with Elijah.

But the free ride didn't last long. Cody kicked the dog off and slammed the door on it. It took two or three slams before the dog finally let go. It fell to the ground with a few strangled yelps and then angry barking as the RV sped away.

"You all right?" Piper shouted back to Elijah

The boy nodded.

"Where to now?" Cody yelled.

"Zach and the motel!"

"Which way?"

"I'm not sure." Piper glanced back and saw that her little brother was pointing to the left. "Are you sure?" she called. "We're supposed to turn left?"

Elijah nodded. Without questioning, Piper threw the RV into a skidding, sharp turn—

"AUUGGHHH!"

—and they headed left.

●

"They're going back to Shadow Man's Compound!" Willard exclaimed as he and the old-timer watched the blip move across the map on the computer screen.

He reached for the keyboard and typed:

Don't go back to Shadow Man's headquarters!

But when he looked at the monitor, he saw that the word *Don't* was somehow missing.

Willard scowled and retyped the word. But the computer was jammed. No matter how many times he tried to type it, the word *Don't* just wouldn't appear.

"What's going on?" the old man asked.

"Your computer is frozen."

"Really?"

Willard kept trying to type the word but had no success.

"That's strange," the man said. And before Willard could stop him, he reached toward the *enter* key

"No," Willard cried, "not that key. It'll send it!"

"What key? This one here?" the hermit asked as he hit the key and sent the message.

"Yeah," Willard sighed in defeat, "that one."

●

Zach had barely managed to get control of the motorcycle when the cell phone began vibrating in his back pocket. He reached in and dug it out. Keeping one eye on the road he read the tiny screen:

go back to Shadow Man's headquarters!

He frowned. It didn't make sense. If there was one place he didn't want to revisit, it was Shadow Man's Compound. Still, the instructions over the cell phone hadn't been wrong yet.

He slid the cell phone into his pocket and threw the bike into a sharp left, heading toward the Compound.

A moment later a pair of headlights bounced onto the road behind him. He glanced over his shoulder. It was Monica and her goons.

He revved the bike faster and roared down the dark road. But no matter how fast he went, the van stayed on his tail

●

Piper peered out the windshield. She didn't believe her eyes. "What have you done?" she shouted back to her little brother.

"What's wrong?" Cody called.

"He's brought us back to the Compound!" she cried. "Elijah, what did you do?!"

The little guy gave no answer except for his usual satisfied grin.

Suddenly, Shadow Man's fortress loomed before them. Piper hit the brakes and slid the RV to a stop just a few yards from the front entrance.

The area was too small to turn around, so she threw the vehicle into reverse. It would have been a good idea, except for the Hummer that suddenly appeared behind them, blocking their path. She wasn't sure how much more abuse the old RV could take, but she had no choice.

She stomped on the gas, preparing to ram the Hummer.

But the RV didn't move. Not an inch. Instead, its wheels just spun in place.

"What's going on?" Cody shouted, his eyes wide and his face white with fear. "Are we stuck?"

She blew the hair out of her eyes and pressed the accelerator harder.

More spinning but no movement.

Her mind raced, trying to understand. There was no mud, no snow. Why couldn't they move?

Suddenly, the side door flew open. She twirled around and had her answer. Shadow Man stood before them, one arm raised toward the RV, holding it in place with his powers.

"Welcome, children," he sneered. "Ssso nice of you to return."

Piper turn to Elijah. The little guy didn't look frightened ... but he was no longer smiling.

●

Dad groaned and tried to move his head, but it seemed to weigh a ton. He forced his eyes open and saw the blur of a hospital room. With lots of effort, he finally rolled his head to the side and saw another bed.

And his wife.

"Juud . . . . . ." . . ." his tongue was so thick no words came. "Juuu . . . . . ." . . ."

He heard a small beep on the other side of him and a nurse's voice. "Doctor, the husband is coming around."

There was another beep, and the doctor's voice answered through the intercom. "It's time for another dose. Give one to both of them."

"Yes, Doctor."

Dad tried to move, but his body felt like lead. He opened his mouth and forced out the word, "No ... "

"It's all right," the nurse said. "You'll be just fine."

"Nooo."

He saw the glint of a needle in the dim light. Desperately, he tried to move — not to save himself, but his wife.

"Steady now."

He felt the tiny burn of the needle.

"No ..."

"There we go."

Once again his eyes grew heavy. No matter how he tried, he could not keep them open. They closed, and the silence returned.

●

The Compound came into Zach's view. So did the Hummer and RV. He immediately hit the brakes. Unfortunately, Monica's van behind him wasn't quite as quick, which would explain the...

SCREETCH!

followed by the

THUD!

of it slamming into the back of Zach's bike and throwing it forward.

Zach yelled as he hung onto the handlebars. He managed to steer clear of the Hummer but had to dump the bike in order to miss the RV. He came to a sliding stop at Shadow Man's feet.

Monica's van wasn't quite so lucky.

It slammed head-on into the rear of the Hummer. Of course, the Hummer was barely scratched, but the van didn't survive as well. Now it looked like a crunched accordion with steam rising from it.

Unfortunately, that didn't stop Monica from prying herself out of the metal accordion and screaming. "You moron! Who taught you to drive?"

"Nobody," Silas said as he stumbled out after her.

"Well, it shows! Where's Bruno?"

There was no answer. She turned back to the van. "Bruno?"

Finally, the big lug crawled out and tumbled to the ground.

Monica raced to him. "Bruno ... Bruno?"

The man was definitely dazed.

"BRUNO!"

He grinned foolishly at her. "That was fun, Mommy. Can we go on the ride again?"

"Silence!" Shadow Man demanded.

Bruno fell silent. So did everyone else.

"You will come with me," he ordered. "And bring the children." Leaning closer to Elijah, he hissed. "And you thought you dessstroyed my Chamber, did you?"

Elijah blinked.

"You did not dessstroy it, my little friend. You have only increasssed itsss range ... ssso everyone can enjoy itsss power!"

Chapter Nine

Testings

Piper sat tied to a chair along with Cody, Zach, and Elijah in Shadow Man's office. They were facing what Shadow Man called the Chamber. Well, it had been a chamber. Now it was a pile of shattered glass. The only part that remained was a circular tube where Piper guessed its ceiling had been. A circular tube that was pulsing orange, red, green ... orange, red, green ... orange, red, green ...

Monica and her thugs had been told to wait in the hall. Now the kids were alone with Shadow Man, whose fingers flew over some sort of computer keyboard.

"You'll like thisss," he hissed. "You'll like it a lot."

Piper leaned over to her brother and whispered. "Got any more plans?"

"Yes," he whispered.

Piper's heart pounded. "Great," she said. "What are they?"

"I think we should escape."

Her hopes soared. "How?"

"I haven't worked out the details."

Her hopes crashed.

She looked back to Shadow Man as he hit a final key and the room exploded with light so intense that, for a moment, she was blinded.

As her eyes adjusted to the brightness, she saw that things had majorly changed.

For starters, Cody sat in an actor's chair holding a movie script. He wore top-of-the-line clothing, sunglasses, and had a smile that revealed dazzlingly perfect teeth. And on a scale of 1 to 10, his body was a definite 11. Around him stood a team of makeup ladies, hairstylists, and about a dozen girls all sighing and begging for his autograph.

Piper frowned and then spotted her brother. He was still his sloppy self (complete with hurricane haircut), but now he was decked out like some sort of multigazillionaire, with gold chain necklaces, bracelets, a diamond studded watch, and a silk suit with wads of money stuffed in the pockets. Pretty amazing.

But not as amazing as what both Zach and Cody stared at. Instead of paying attention to how they'd been transformed, they were both gawking at . . .

Her!

At first she didn't understand, thinking something was wrong. But when she looked down at herself, she saw that *nothing* was wrong. Nothing at all! She no longer saw the scrawny, all-knees-and-elbows tomboy who hid under extra-large baggy sweatshirts. Now she had the looks and shape of a model—a supermodel. Tall and lean, with all the right curves in all the right places. No wonder they stared. She looked fantastic! And, as she swished her thick blonde hair to the side, she felt fantastic.

"Ssso," Shadow Man hissed. "You like?"

Zach was the first to speak. "Are you kidding?" Zach said, pulling out a thick wad of cash. "What's not to like?!"

Shadow Man grinned. "Yesss. Thisss and ssso much more will be yoursss as sssoon as your brother decccidesss."

Piper turned to Elijah. Unlike the others, he was exactly as he had been. No fancy clothes. No fancy body. No fancy anything.

"What's wrong?" she asked her little brother. "Why haven't you changed?"

Shadow Man answered for him. "Your brother isss a ssstuborn one. He refusssesss all that I offer."

Piper frowned, not understanding.

"Yet that will change," Shadow Man said. He reached back to the keyboard, and once again his fingers flew. When he'd finished, he looked up grinning. "Yesss, that will change very sssoon."

With a flourish, he hit the final key and more light flooded the room—light so bright that Piper had to cover her eyes. When she finally removed her hands, she gasped.

Now they all stood on a giant stage the size of a football field and at least fifty feet high. Below them, stretched out as far as she could see, were people. Thousands of them, no, millions. They were all looking up and chanting her name: "Piper ... Piper ... Piper ..."

It was unbelievable.

She immediately glanced down to make sure she still

had her incredible body. And, of course, she did. Cody and Zach were across the stage, checking. themselves out, equally as pleased.

But where was Elijah? Where had he—

And then she saw him. At the very center of the stage, sitting on a throne.

To his right, Shadow Man sat on another, grinning and laughing.

Piper glided toward them, as graceful as any runway model, while thousands of adoring fans continued calling her name.

"What's going on?" she shouted.

Shadow Man didn't hear. He was too busy yelling to Elijah. "Thisss can all be yoursss! You can help me rule the world! Together we will sshare all itsss power and glory!"

But Elijah seemed totally unimpressed.

Shadow Man leaned forward. "What about your brother and sssissster? You would deprive them of such joy?"

Elijah hesitated.

Shadow Man nodded. "That'sss right. If you won't do it for yourssself, then do it for them."

Elijah swallowed, then looked out over the crowd as their chanting grew louder.

"All you need do isss ssubmit, and they will be given thisss. Thisss and ssso much more."

Piper wasn't sure what Shadow Man meant, but she couldn't imagine her little brother turning all this down. How could he? Everything was so incredible! And if he wasn't interested, then it was true, he should at least think about Zach and her.

Still, Elijah hesitated. He turned toward Zach, who was eating up the money and worship like a starving man gobbling up food. And, speaking of food, there were at least a dozen tables surrounding him, all filled with his favorite meals: chips, pizza, chips, steak, chips, ice cream, and more chips.

It was true, Zach loved to eat. He loved in-between-meal snacks, and in-between in-between snacks, and in-between, in-between, in-between ... well, you get the idea. This was the happiest Piper had ever seen him. All that food plus the fame plus the money. For him, it was a dream come true. To be honest, it was also a dream come true for her.

Yet Elijah still hesitated. What was wrong with him?

The boy turned back to his sister. She motioned to her fantastic body, to the millions of people loving and adoring her, to everything that surrounded them. Surely, he wouldn't deny them this.

But instead of nodding in agreement, a deep sadness filled Elijah's eyes. She didn't understand. How could he be sad when all this could be theirs? Unless...

She turned to Shadow Man. "Is this some sort of trick?" she shouted. "Another one of your lies?"

"No, my dear. I ssswear by all that isss unholy, what you sssee before you isss truth."

"What's the catch?" she shouted.

"There isss no catch. If your brother followsss the Massster, thisss isss the truth of your future."

Suddenly, a voice thundered.

"Truth?"

Piper spun back to Elijah. She knew it was his voice, but it was a thousand times more powerful. Weirder still, when he spoke, his mouth didn't move.

"You call this truth?"

For a moment, Shadow Man seemed surprised. But he quickly recovered. "Yesss, if you follow the Massster."

"No. This is only part of the truth."

It took Piper a moment to find her own voice. "What?" she squeaked. "What do you mean?"

"Here is the complete truth."

Instantly, Piper found herself inside a magnificent palace. Handsome men and beautiful women were waiting upon her. Two were on their knees massaging her feet, giving her the world's greatest pedicure. Two more were at her hands giving her a manicure. Someone else was rubbing her neck. Another, was giving her a facial. She'd never felt so good in her life and couldn't help but sigh with pleasure. If this was "complete truth," sign her up.

She open her eyes and spotted Cody across the marble room. He held another movie script and wore a silk robe as a dozen servants waited on him. But he had changed. Instead of being young and gorgeous, he was now old and ugly. Instead of being his kind, thoughtful self, he was screaming, "I wanted this robe in white! Not ivory! WHITE!"

"But my lord—" one of his servants answered.

"No buts!" Cody yelled. "And tell the director I expect to play *all* the parts in this movie. Do you understand me? ALL!" To make his point, he threw the script at the servant.

"Yes, your highness." The servant bowed low and backed out.

Piper couldn't believe what she saw. And when Cody spotted her staring, he screamed, "What are you looking at?" Before she could answer, he yelled, "Get out of here, or you'll miss your weekly plastic surgery!"

Piper scowled, not understanding.

"And don't frown. You know how that makes wrinkles."

Instinctively, her hands shot to her face. Her skin felt as taut as a rubber band about to snap. She spotted a mirror and motioned one of her servants to hand it to her. When she looked into it, she practically gagged. It was hard to tell her age because, staring back at her, was a creepy clown face, her skin pulled so tight from so many plastic surgeries that it was frozen in a grotesque perma-grin. The only thing worse was her giant-sausage lips from too many lip implants. Then there was her skeleton body. Not a trace of fat could be seen—only bones that jutted out. Finally, the skin that stretched over her arms, legs, and stomach was covered in scars from a hundred surgeries where they had cut and removed the slightest hint of flab. In her attempts to remain beautiful, she'd become a monster.

Behind her, in the mirror's reflection, she saw Zach lying on a couch. At least she thought it was Zach. She spun around and looked at her brother. His lean body had morphed into a ton of blubber with so much fat that she could barely see his face.

He was also yelling, "Make sure there's more chocolate in the next bite of pizza you chew for me!"

Piper looked on, trying not to retch. It was true, Zach was so rich and lazy that he actually hired other people to chew his food for him. They would take a bite of whatever food he commanded, chew it for him, and, you guessed it, spit it into his mouth so all he had to do was swallow it.

"And that is only the beginning."

Elijah's voice was speaking again.

"Here is the future. Here is the final truth."

The scene changed again. Suddenly, they were all standing on a cliff overlooking an ocean of fire. The heat was so intense that it made Piper's eyes water. And the smell reminded her of the time Dad cremated the hamburgers on the barbecue. The only thing worse was the screaming.

Screaming from the people who were burning in the fire.

She spun to Elijah and shouted, "I don't understand!"

"If you wish, I will agree and follow his master."

"And this will be the future?" Piper asked in a small voice.

Elijah said nothing.

Piper looked back to the people and the fire.

Elijah spoke again.

"This is the future for all who chose to follow Shadow Man and his master to their final truth."

"Final truth?" she repeated. "Would it also be yours?" She looked to Elijah. "If you followed, would this also be *your* future?"

He said nothing.

She tried again. "Are you saying that if you follow him, this would be *your* final truth?"

Elijah hesitated a moment, and then slowly began to nod.

Piper shuddered and stepped back. "No!" She closed her eyes against the screaming below. Louder and more strongly, she shouted, "No way! Absolutely not!"

Suddenly, she was back in her young, supermodel body, standing next to her movie-star boyfriend and her filthy rich brother.

"Are you sssure?" Shadow Man, who now stood beside her, hissed.

"Yes, I'm sure! Of course, I'm sure!"

"Really? Because I have ssso much to offer."

Once again she found herself standing on the giant stage beside her brother's throne. Once again millions were shouting her name. For the briefest moment, she hesitated then caught herself. "No!" She closed her eyes again. "Don't do it, Elijah!" She turned to him. "It's not worth it! Don't do it!"

Elijah stared at her a long moment. It was almost like he could see inside her, like he knew what she was thinking. Maybe he could.

When he was satisfied she was telling the truth, he gave another nod.

Suddenly, they were back in Shadow Man's office. There was more blinding light, only this time it came from the tube in the Chamber's ceiling. It was exploding, filling the room with smoke and a thousand sparks.

"What have you done?" Shadow Man screamed. "What have you done?"

Chapter Ten
Wrapping Up

When he heard Shadow Man's cry, the ever-faithful Bruno barged in from the hallway. "What is it, Boss?! What's ..."

That was as far as he got before he stumbled over Shadow Man and fell onto—"Oaff!"—Zach.

The good news was he didn't break any of Zach's bones. The better news was he *did* break Zach's chair. It hit the ground and broke into dozens of pieces, loosening Zach's ropes and allowing him to scramble free.

Bruno jumped up and would have nabbed him, but Bruno was too busy getting tangled up in the rope and falling over what was left of the chair—again and again. This gave Zach plenty of time to untie Cody and Piper, who managed to untie Elijah.

"Grab them!" Shadow Man kept shouting. "Grab them! Grab them!"

"Them?" Bruno cried in confusion. "Which them?"

A good question since, by now, they were all free and racing out into the hallway.

"Ssstop!"

At one end of the hallway stood a door leading outside. Unfortunately, that was also the end where Monica and Silas were sacked out on a bench catching some sleep.

Zach motioned the other direction. "This way!"

They all started to follow—except Elijah.

"Elijah?" Piper whispered. "What is it?"

"Come on, little guy," Zach urged.

But he shook his head and pointed the opposite direction, toward the door and past Monica.

"Forget it," Zach whispered. "It's too dangerous."

Again Elijah shook his head and motioned.

"No way."

"Zach," Piper whispered. "He's never been wrong before."

"Come on," Zach repeated and started forward.

But Piper didn't budge.

Neither did Cody.

Zach turned back and whispered, "Are you guys nuts?"

"Yeah," Cody agreed. "Probably a little. But your sister's right: he's never been wrong." With that he turned and started toward Elijah. Piper followed.

"Cody!" Zach hissed. "Piper!"

But they kept right on walking. Finally, with a heavy sigh, he turned and followed.

They continued down the hall as quietly as they could. Unfortunately, it wasn't quiet enough. They were right in front of Monica when she opened one eye. Then the other. "What's going on?" she demanded.

But instead of answering, Zach had better idea. "Run!"

This time everyone agreed.

Monica leaped to her feet and was joined by Silas.

"Stop!" he shouted, pulling a weapon from his coat. "I've got a gun!"

The door lay ten yards ahead.

"We'll never make it!" Piper yelled.

But then she heard Bruno lumber into the hallway behind them—still dragging the rope and pieces of chair.

"Hang on," he shouted, "I'm coming!"

"No!" Monica cried.

"Don't worry, I'll help!"

"No, no, no!"

Fortunately, Bruno's idea of helping included arriving and tripping over his rope.

"Oaff!" he cried as he fell over Silas.

"Oaff!" Silas cried as he fell over Monica.

"You fools!" Monica screeched as they all crashed to the floor.

Cody was the first to arrive at the door. He threw it open and held it for Piper and the others to escape.

Once outside, they raced to the RV just yards away.

"Hurry!" Zach shouted as Piper climbed inside.

Elijah and Cody followed. And finally Zach. He slipped into the driver's seat behind the wheel. (Piper felt no need to volunteer for the job.)

The door to the building flew open.

Well, it *started* to fly open. But after only a foot it suddenly stopped. Piper could see Monica and her thugs trying to squeeze through, but for some unknown reason, it was stuck. Then again, maybe the reason wasn't so unknown. Because as Piper looked over to her little brother, she saw him concentrating very hard on that very door.

Meanwhile, Zach was trying to start the engine.

"Come on, baby," he coaxed, "come on, come on." But nothing happened. He shouted over his shoulder. "Piper, pray!"

"What?"

"You heard me, pray!"

Normally, she wasn't crazy about praying in front of people, especially when "people" also included Cody. But since she was even less crazy about dying, she gave it a shot. She bowed her head and began. "Dear God, help us get out of here."

As she prayed, Zach tried the engine again.

Nothing.

"Please Lord, we really, really need to—"

Suddenly, the RV fired up. "Amen!" Zach shouted.

"Amen!" the others agreed.

Zach dropped the vehicle into reverse and it jerked backwards—throwing Piper forward into Cody's arms ... just like old times.

"Sorry!" she blurted.

"No problem." He helped her back up and smiled.

"Hang on!" Zach dropped the RV into drive, cranked the wheel hard, and hit the gas. This time Cody fell into Piper's arms.

"Sorry!" he laughed.

She tried to return the laugh, but it came out more of a nervous quack ... just like old times.

They bounced onto the dirt road and picked up speed.

"Are they coming?" Zach called.

Cody glanced out the back. "Not yet."

"They will," Zach said, "they will."

"Where to now?" Cody asked.

"Mom and Dad."

"We don't even know where they are," Piper argued. "How can we expect to find them?"

For once in his life, Zach had no answer.

No one did.

Except Elijah. The little guy was crawling up into the seat behind the table with the computer.

"What's up, buddy?" Piper asked. "You don't know how to work that thing."

It was true, he didn't. But he did know how to point.

Piper traded glances with Cody then moved into the seat beside her little brother to take a look.

●

"All right!" Willard cheered as they watched the blip move across the computer screen. "They're getting away!"

"Excellent," the hermit agreed.

Without a word, Willard reached for the keyboard and began to type.

"What are you doing?" the old man asked.

"Giving them instructions on how to pick me up." But he barely started before another address appeared on the screen:

Johnsonville Hospital, 278 North Hampshire

"Where did that come from?" Willard asked.

The old timer scratched his head. "Hmm," was all he said.

Suddenly Willard reached over and hit the *enter* key to send it.

"What are you doing?" the hermit asked.

Willard cut him a look. "Just saving you the effort," he sighed.

Epilogue

You let them get away?

Shadow Man felt the voice more than he heard it. But that was how it always happened here, deep in the cavern under the Compound. Here, where the Master made his abode.

"Not for long," Shadow Man thought back his reply

Good, came the response. *I would hate to be disappointed. You know how I hate disappointment.*

Shadow Man knew full well how the Master hated disappointment. Over the centuries he had seen first hand how his fellow creatures had been tortured and destroyed. Actually, not destroyed, but tortured and imprisoned in the lake of fire. A fate so horrendous that they *wished* they had been destroyed.

Suddenly, Shadow Man felt the Master's invisible fingers grab his throat and lift him high into the air.

"Yesss," Shadow Man choked, "I know, I know how you hate disssappointment ... "

In an instant, he was flung into the air, flying across the giant cave until he hit the icy stone wall and slumped to the ground.

The time of The Enemy's Appearance will soon arrive. We must prevent the boy and his partner from warning the others.

"Partner?" Shadow Man asked as he struggled back to his feet. "There isss another?"

According to The Book, there will be two. They will oppose me and call down the Enemy's judgments from Heaven. But you will not let that happen.

"No, Sssir," Shadow Man said, "absssolutely not."

Good, good. Now, tell me of your plan.

"Plan?" Shadow Man asked.

Suddenly he felt the cold fingers around his throat.

"Oh yesss, the plan, the plan, of courssse."

The fingers released, waiting.

Shadow Man's mind raced, trying to think of something. "We know they are going to ressscue the parentsss."

There was no reply.

Taking that as a good sign, Shadow Man continued. "I will sssummon darker forcesss to pursssue them."

Again there was silence.

Another good sign.

"Right now, right thisss sssecond I will releassse them. I will order them to begin closssing in."

A chill spread through the layers of fat in his body. The Master was moving. To where, Shadow Man did not know. But he knew it was away. And he knew something else:

He must not fail again. He would use all of his powers to make sure that did not happen. If he did not ... he shuddered, refusing to think of the consequences, refusing to think what could only be his fiery future.

"How much farther?" Zach called from behind the wheel.

Piper stared at the computer screen. "Three, maybe four miles."

"Are they behind us yet?" Zach asked.

Cody looked out the back window. "Still no sign of them."

"Maybe we lost them," Piper said hopefully.

"Maybe," Zach said, though it was obvious he didn't believe it. Glancing into the rearview mirror, he spoke to Elijah. The boy sat beside Piper, quietly humming away. "Sure wish you felt like giving me some more clues, little guy."

"Clues?" Piper asked.

"Yeah. When we were in Shadow Man's office, Elijah was talking to me like a mile a minute."

"To you?" Cody said.

"Yeah. He was showing me the future, testing me to see if I wanted to follow Shadow Man."

"You were being tested?" Piper said. "I was the one being tested. He was talking to *me"*

"Yeah, right," Zach laughed. "He was talking to me the whole time. In fact, he even took me to a fiery lake and said that was Shadow Man's final truth, whatever that means."

Piper's jaw dropped. "He showed me the same thing."

"No way."

"Guys ..." Cody tried interrupting.

"He sure did," Piper argued. "And he showed me a

giant stage and a palace and what we could look like if we . . . "

"Guys . . . "

"That's what he showed *me.*"

"GUYS!"

Piper and Zach turned to Cody.

He cleared his throat a little embarrassed. "Actually that's what he was showing me, too."

All their eyes slowly turned to her little brother. The RV grew very, very silent — except for the hymn Elijah was humming softly. Was it possible? Had they all been through the same test? Each one, without the others knowing it?

"Hey, check it out," Zach exclaimed. Something in the night sky had caught his attention, and he craned his head for a better look.

Piper and Cody moved to a nearby window to see.

At first Piper thought they were black, swirling clouds. But as she looked closer, she saw they weren't clouds at all, but crows. Thousands of them. All circling the RV.

"What's that about?" Cody asked.

"Do you think . . . " Piper kept her eyes glued to the window. "Do you think they're coming after us?"

"Relax," Zach said. "They're just crows."

"Yeah." Piper swallowed and gave a nervous nod. "Just crows."

"Except . . . " Cody said.

She turned to him and he continued, "When was the last time you ever saw crows fly at night?"

Piper looked back out the window. The sky swarmed with darkness — so thick it blotted out the stars.

"I wonder what's going on?" Zach said.

Piper threw another look to Elijah. She wished she hadn't.

Beads of perspiration had formed on his face. And, instead of humming, his lips had started to silently move, as if ... as if he were praying.

Zach saw him too. "You all right? Elijah, everything okay?"

But Elijah didn't answer. Instead, he closed his eyes and continued moving his lips.

Piper watched. She wasn't sure what was next. It probably would be tough and pretty scary. Still, from what they had been through, she knew they would be safe. Whatever was out there could frighten them, yes. And it could definitely put them to the test. But if they kept obeying and staying connected to God, then whatever evil they faced would never be able to harm them. That much she knew.

So, like her little brother, Piper Dawkins bowed her head and started to pray.

Seriously Sick Bible Stuff

by Ed Strauss
art by Erwin Haya

Introduction

Ever heard someone say, "I wish I could've lived during Bible times"? Or maybe your kid sister sighs, "If only I could've followed Jesus around." Chances are she's read too many picture books showing Jesus and his disciples in clean robes with shampooed hair strolling through sunny orchards. Butterflies flutter by and happy children skip through fields of flowers. No one is stepping in donkey dung.

Riiight. But when night hits, and your sister learns that "the Son of Man has no place to lay his head" (Matthew 8:20) — meaning everybody's *sleeping* in the orchard — she'll jump in her time machine and zap back to the twenty-first century. Most girls couldn't hack ancient Israel even if they had a *house* to sleep in. Don't laugh. Most boys couldn't either.

Life during Bible times was like growing up in a Third World country. A lot of boys today are spoiled. You're used to fresh food in the fridge, your own bedroom, hours of playtime every day, showers (when you clue in that you're dirty), and clean toilets to sit on. Take away your tacos, toys, TVs, and toilets, plunge into Bible days, and you'd go into shock.

Oh sure, large Roman cities had theaters, clean water, and sewage systems. Yeah, yeah, and the rich had fine clothes, feasts, and read poetry while slaves manicured their toenails. *But!* We're not talking about Roman cities here. We're talking about Israel, where most Jews lived in dusty villages and crowded towns and no one was manicuring their toenails. Toilets? They squatted over stinking, fly-infested holes in the yard.

For over a thousand years, from the time of Joshua till the time of Jesus, things barely changed in the land of Israel. These days somebody's always inventing something new. Back then there was hardly any new technology. There were no flat-screen TVs, no computer games, and no DVDs. There were no skateboards or bicycles. After a day's work, the Israelites sat around telling stories and playing games like checkers. And, well . . . that was *about it*.

Changed your mind? Don't wanna visit ancient Israel? Sorry, it's too late. You've already started reading. Now all you can do is pack your bags and prepare for time travel. You're going to get a look at what life was *really* like during Bible times. Don't forget the toilet paper. You'll *need* it. You won't see another roll for two—maybe three—thousand years.

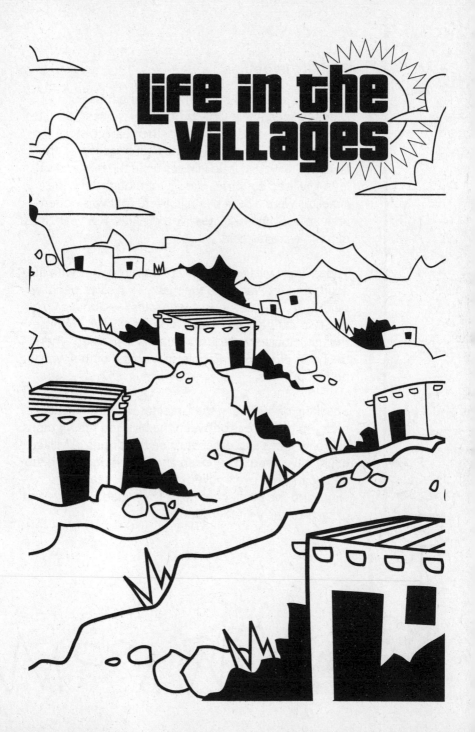

Life in the Villages

Hillbilly Israelites

Israel was a skinny chunk of land along the Mediterranean Sea. Only problem was, most Israelites never saw the sea. For much of their early history, the Philistines controlled all the best beaches, so the Israelites stayed in little villages up in the hills and valleys. Civilized countries like Egypt thought that the Israelites were a bunch of hillbillies. That was not entirely true. Some Israelites lived in cities. But yeah, *most* of them were farmers.

The average village had about twenty houses with fifty adults and fifty kids. Do the math. That's five people per house, and the houses were *small* — about as big as a two-car garage. People didn't really *live* in houses though. Houses were just a safe place to sleep where the bears didn't bite. People spent most of their waking hours outdoors.

Speaking of outdoors, the Israelites planted wheat and barley in the valleys between the hills and grew grapes and olive trees and other stuff on the slopes. A village might have about forty oxen and three hundred sheep and goats. The oxen pulled plows, the sheep grew wool, and the goats gave milk. They used donkeys and oxcarts to carry stuff around.

Mud-Brick Houses

Most houses were made of dried mud bricks. The walls were so weak you could dig a hole through them with your hands — and some guys *did!* Rain wore holes in the walls too. The nasty news is that poisonous snakes sometimes lived in those holes. Yikes!

In Jesus' day, houses probably had only one or two rooms and almost zero privacy. Doorways were so narrow and low that adults had to bend down to en-

ter. Israelites didn't have too many windows either, so it was usually dark inside, except for the light of smoky oil lamps. The floor was made out of dirt — or clay if you could afford it.

Larger homes might have had four rooms. The open courtyard with a wall around it was "room" number one. Your mom ground grain, cooked, and wove cloth here, and everyone ate here. Your ox slept in room number two, the covered porch on the east wall. That's also where the plow and tools were stored. The family slept in room three on the west wall. Room four against the back wall was for food storage.

Simple, Bare Necessities

Okay, by now you've clued in that living in ancient Israel means things were basic. Well, *how* basic? Running water? Not a chance. Your mom or sister had to lug jugs of water from the village well. In wealthy homes you washed your feet before you trotted in the house, but only if the floor had tiles. In farmhouses, floors were just hard-packed dirt, so washing your feet was pointless.

Want a shower? Sure, stand in the courtyard and pour water on yourself. Yup, that will work.

Toilets? Oh right, *toilets*. Your bathroom was a stinking pit out in the courtyard. It buzzed so loud with flies it sounded like a beehive. You really had to keep the lid on that sucker.

FUN FACT:

Toilet paper didn't exist in ancient Israel. It didn't even exist in America until Joseph Gayetty invented it in 1857. Before then, people wiped with pages from mail order catalogs. Of course, they didn't have catalogs in ancient Israel, so, um, what did they use? Whatever they could find: their bare left hand, rags, wool, stones, and sticks. You name it. Most people preferred leaves. Some of the farm trees must've been almost leafless.

Oodles of Kids

Houses were small, but the more kids your mom had, the more blessed she felt she was. If she had ten boys running around, she thought that was just great. A guy named Heman had fourteen sons and three daughters (1 Chronicles 25:5). Some *he-man*, huh? You're wondering *why* so many kids, right? Just wait. We'll talk about chores soon enough.

Leaky Roofs

Roofs on the mud houses were flat. Branches or thorn bushes were laid on wood rafters, and clay was packed on top of that. These roofs were strong enough to walk on, but if you jumped on them, you'd knock holes in them. Can't you just hear Jewish moms telling their kids, "Joab! How many times must I *tell* you? Do *not* jump on the roof!"

Roofs weren't hard to tear apart either. Once Jesus was inside a crowded house, and four guys wanted him to heal their sick friend. When couldn't get to him, they ripped a big hole in the roof and lowered their buddy down to Jesus with ropes (Mark 2:1 – 4).

On hot summer nights the whole family slept up on the roof because the breeze made it cooler. People went up there to pray too. They even stored food there. Some rooftops were so cluttered with stuff that you could hide up there. Play hide-and-seek and you just *know* somebody's on the roof.

One problem was that when it rained during winter, the clay on the roof would wash away, and people in the house below got a shower! Leaky roofs had to be fixed all the time. And after all that rain, *grass* even grew on the rooftops!

Tunics and Cloaks

Jewish men wore a light robe called a tunic. It was made out of wool or linen and reached down to the ankles. When you were working—which was usually—you tucked it up into your belt. Some guys said, "Aw! Forget *this*!" and just wore short tunics all the time.

Men wore a cloak over the tunic. The cloak was made of thick wool, and it was like a blanket, so on hot days you slung it over your shoulder. When you sat down in the dirt, you folded it and used it as a rug. When you went to sleep, the dirty rug became your blanket.

When the prophet Elijah was caught up to heaven in a whirlwind, his cloak blew off—not surprising with all that wind. When it hit the ground, his buddy, Elisha, picked it up and wore it. He *needed* it! After all, he'd just finished tearing his own clothes apart (2 Kings 2:11 – 13).

Designer Duds and Underpants

Some people think that Jesus wore expensive designer clothes because his tunic was seamless, woven in one piece from top to bottom (John 19:23). Nuh-uh. Many tunics from Galilee were woven in one piece. It was standard issue. That was how they made tunics in Galilee.

Jesus was no fashion show. After all, he was the one who said, "Do not worry . . . about your body, what you will wear" (Matthew 6:25). The rich Pharisees? Yeah, now *these* guys were the ones wearing fancy clothes.

By the way, the Bible calls Jesus' tunic his "undergarment." This is not talking about his underwear. People back then wore loincloths for underpants. *Undergarment* just means the tunic *under* his cloak. You know, like a T-shirt under a sweater.

Buying Stuff

Most boys get bored out of their skulls when Mom drags them to the mall to buy them clothes. Be thankful you didn't go out shopping in Bible times. Back then there were no price tags, so Mom might stand there arguing with a merchant over the price *for an hour*. They'd argue, haggle, and even yell at each other — and enjoy every minute of it! Ain't it great to live in the day of price tags?

Clean Clothes, Anyone?

Farmers weren't big on washing clothes because it was hard work to wash them by hand. Besides, it wore clothes out if you whacked them against the rocks *too* much. (Yep! That's how Moms washed clothes. *Smack! Whack! Splak!*) Anyway, the day after Mom washed your clothes, they started getting dirty again. And it's *not* like you had several sets of clothing. You wore the same tunic day after day and even slept in it.

Bedtime! What Fun!

There were no beds as we know them. You lay on a straw mat right on the dirt floor and covered yourself with your cloak. Most families slept on the floor together, so if you had to get up in the middle of the night for any reason, you ended up stepping on everyone else.

Israelites considered dogs so disgusting they wouldn't even *own* one, let alone keep one in the house. But farm animals? Sure. Every night Dad brought the milk goat into the house to sleep. (You're asking *why*, right? So no one stole it. Plus, the extra body heat kept the house warm.)

Apart from the smell, animals don't care where they poop. Goats will happily drop loads of dung balls just about anywhere. If you were an Israelite boy, guess whose job it would be to clean out the poop in the morning?

Just so this doesn't *totally* gross you out, the family slept on a floor eighteen inches higher than where the animals slept. This prevented poop balls from rolling across the floor to your sleeping mat. Makes a guy look forward to summer nights when you could sleep on the *roof*, huh?

Ash Heaps and Trash

Ovens were made of clay or stone and were usually outside in the courtyard. After all, your mom wouldn't want the house to smell like *smoke*, right? But when rainy season came, you had to cook indoors. Then things got smoky. Eventually the smoke escaped out a window.

Household trash? When the oven got full of ashes, Mom scraped them out and dumped them in a pile behind the house, along with broken pottery. When poor Job ended up covered with pus-filled boils, he went out behind his house, "took a piece of broken pottery and scraped himself with it as he sat among the ashes" (Job 2:8).

WHAT TO DO WITH THE DOO?

You have four guesses as to what happened to all the goat, donkey, sheep, and ox poo.

It was

(a) packed around the fruit trees

(b) dumped in a big ol' heap in the yard

(c) dried and used as fuel

(d) dumped into the toilet with the human excrement

If you guessed (a), you are *so* right! Jesus talked about a farmer fertilizing a fig tree. In the original Greek, *fertilize* means "to cast dung" (Luke 13:8). Wow! They *threw* the stuff? One of the biggest blessings farmers wanted was to sit peacefully under a fig tree and think (Micah 4:4). You'd wanna pick a tree that hadn't been dunged recently.

If you guessed (b), you are also right! Dung ended up in the dunghill. These days the polite term is *manure pile*. The Israelites sometimes beefed up their valuable fertilizer by trampling straw in it with their feet. In Isaiah 25:10–11, God says the Moabites would "spread out their *hands* in it, as a swimmer spreads out his hands to swim." Hey! Wanna be on the Moabite swim team in the Bronze Age Olympics?

If you guessed (c), the answer is *also correct*. When God told Ezekiel to burn human poop and Ezekiel got grossed out, God told him he could cook his food over flaming cow manure instead (Ezekiel 4:15).

The only wrong answer in this quiz was (d). Toss animal dung down the toilet with human waste. C'mon! That's wasteful!

GET SMARTER

The Hebrew word *Madmenah* means "Dunghill," and it was similiar to the names of two Israelite towns named Madmannah (See Joshua 15:31 and Isaiah 10:31). Some Bible scholars say these were fertilizer-producing centers. You'd think that only a madman would live in Madmannah, but hey, they had loads of dung. Why throw the stuff away when you can sell it?

On the other hand, smart Israelites found work elsewhere. Only the most desperate people took such filthy jobs. The Bible says God lifts the needy "out of the dunghill" (Psalm 113:7, *KJV*). It was the kind of job you prayed God would get you *out* of.

Don't want to live in Manure Pile? Hey, like your parents say, if you want a *good* job when you grow up, study hard now. Sometimes school is boring, but it's even more boring to have a dead-end job and low wages for the rest of your life.

The Malls of Hazor

There were no shopping malls in Bible times, but there *were* shops. Every so often there was a city, and cities had market streets. Spend a day in town and, wow, you got to see shops of carpenters, mat weavers, potters, bakers, cheese makers, goldsmiths, or farmers selling vegetables. Exciting, huh?

Of course, cities back then were pretty small. Little ones covered only an acre or two and had a few hundred people. (That's a *city*? Yup.) A world-class city like Hazor spread over 175 acres and had a population of 40,000. Ho! *Monster* metropolis or what?

Back then, cities usually sat on a hill and had high stone walls. Being on a hill was a must. You never could tell when an enemy army might want to try attacking you. (Yeah, to rob your fancy "mall.")

Sometimes the markets had more than just cheese and bread. Sometimes there was stuff from other countries. Israel was on the caravan roads between Syria and Egypt, and camels constantly plodded through, loaded with spices and silk and perfume and all kinds of high-priced goodies.

When is Garbage Day?

There are, um, some things about ancient cities you should know. Like, they were usually crowded and had narrow streets and alleys zigzagging all over the place. Worse yet, there was no garbage collection. It was like a permanent New York City garbage strike. So where did rubbish end up? If it was small stuff, it got chucked into the alleys. Folks weren't particular back then and there weren't laws against littering. But if, say, your goat died, it's not like you could get away with dumping it in the street. You had to haul *that* away.

The Local Dump

Jerusalem had a huge, open, stinky garbage dump just outside the city in the Valley of Hinnom (Gehenna). All day and all night long, fires burned the garbage, popping and sizzling and sending up foul-smelling smoke. Usually the wind carried the smoke away, but sometimes it blew back toward the city.

The Gehenna Dump was just swarming with flies, and fly maggots squirmed in and out of rotting food and oozing dead things and dung. The Gehenna Dump was so bad that Jesus used it to describe what *hell* was like — a place where "their worm does not die, and the fire is not quenched" (Mark 9:47 – 48).

NOT-SO-FUN FACT:

Sometimes enemy armies surrounded ancient cities and besieged them for years, not letting anyone in or out. When the people inside the city ran out of food and water, they might be forced to eat their own dung and drink their own urine.

(See Isaiah 36:12.)

The Dung Gate

The dump was just outside the *Dung Gate*, and if that doesn't give you an idea of the kind of make-you-gag garbage that was dragged through it, nothing will. Rubbish, garbage, carcasses, dung, you name it.

You gotta wonder what Nehemiah was thinking when he sent the choir out singing. He said, "I also assigned two large choirs to give thanks. One was to proceed on top of the wall to the right, toward the Dung Gate" (Nehemiah 12:31). Well, they had just *rebuilt* the Dung Gate, so it didn't stink so badly yet. Otherwise the singers might've gagged and fallen off the wall.

Sewage in the City

You won't find it in the New International Version — the translators were too polite — but the King James Version of the Bible talks six times about men urinating against the city walls (1 Kings 14:10). You just *gotta* know that with thousands of men and boys watering the walls every day—get a few sunny days in a row and, *Whoooeeee!*—them walls would reek!

Back then, most Israelite cities had no sewage systems—just open gutters that ran along alleys. These yellow streams trickled down the streets. Israel was dry and dusty, so when Isaiah 10:6 talks about "mud in the streets," it's not necessarily talking about rain mixing with dust to make this (ahem) "mud."

And were you wondering where city folks did "number two"? They had toilets in their courtyards. If you wonder what on earth they did when their toilets got full, well, we won't even go there.

PUBLIC LATRINES

Derek Dundee of Mallabassa, Missouri asks: "Did Israelite men only pee on walls? That's gross!" No, Derek, if a building was torn down, guys would urinate among the rubble too. After King Jehu demolished the temple of Baal, the Israelites used it as a public latrine (urinal) for hundreds of years (2 Kings 10:27). Must've been real stinky by that time, 'cause, like, no one ever cleaned it!

Street Cleaners

There were no garbage men or street cleaners in ancient Israel — not *human* at least. But ever see a nature show where buzzards are gulping down a rotten corpse and the narrator says, "The vulture is the garbage collector of Africa"? And jackals are such good scavengers that they're called "street cleaners" in many African cities.

Back in Israel, the cleaning crews were canines. The dogs of the day looked like dirty coyotes. They prowled around the cities, half wild, as they ate garbage. As far as the dogs were concerned, there wasn't *enough* garbage, and they often wandered around howling and looking for food. It's a good thing they *did* clean the streets! That's where little boys and girls played (Zechariah 8:5)!

Get Stronger

Does your bedroom look like some alley in ancient Israel? If there are dirty duds ditched on the floor and discolored underpants decorating the doorknobs, you need to do some serious "street cleaning." (Don't count on any wild dogs doing the job for you.)

Worse yet, does your room look like the Jerusalem dump, with mold growing on plates of abandoned spaghetti under your bed, and maggots crawling through half-eaten peaches? Listen, an important part of being a man is keeping things neat. God told King Hezekiah that the most important job he had to do before he died was to put his house in order (2 Kings 20:1). So why not start with your heart and then tackle your room?

NIV Adventure Bible

Softcover • ISBN 9780310715436

In this revised edition of the *NIV Adventure Bible*, kids 9-12 will discover the treasure of God's Word. Filled with great adventures and exciting features, the *NIV Adventure Bible* opens a fresh new encounter with Scripture for kids, especially at a time when they are trying to develop their own ideas and opinions independent of their parents.

Available now at your local bookstore!

We want to hear from you. Please send your comments about this book to us in care of zreview@zondervan.com. Thank you.

ZONDERVAN.com/
AUTHORTRACKER
follow your favorite authors